DOCTOR WHO

ONLY HUMAN

The Doctor Who *50th Anniversary Collection*

Ten Little Aliens
Stephen Cole

Dreams of Empire
Justin Richards

Last of the Gaderene
Mark Gatiss

Festival of Death
Jonathan Morris

Fear of the Dark
Trevor Baxendale

Players
Terrance Dicks

Remembrance of the Daleks
Ben Aaronovitch

EarthWorld
Jacqueline Rayner

Only Human
Gareth Roberts

Beautiful Chaos
Gary Russell

The Silent Stars Go By
Dan Abnett

DOCTOR WHO

ONLY HUMAN

GARETH ROBERTS

BBC
BOOKS

1 3 5 7 9 10 8 6 4 2

First published in 2005 by BBC Worldwide Ltd.
This edition published in 2013 by BBC Books, an imprint of Ebury Publishing.
A Random House Group Company

Doctor Who is a BBC Wales production for BBC One.
Executive producers: Steven Moffat and Caroline Skinner

The Random House Group Limited Reg. No. 954009
Addresses for companies within the Random House Group can be found at
www.randomhouse.co.uk

A CIP catalogue record for this book is available from the British Library.

ISBN 978 1 849 90519 0

Editorial director: Albert DePetrillo
Editorial manager: Nicholas Payne
Series consultant: Justin Richards
Project editor: Steve Tribe
Cover design: Two Associates © Woodlands Books Ltd, 2012
Production: Alex Goddard

Printed and bound in the USA

To buy books by your favourite authors and register for offers,
visit www.randomhouse.co.uk

INTRODUCTION

It was my first time back in the saddle of *Doctor Who* fiction for many years. Nine years, in fact. Nine years mainly spent in the world of television soap opera. I'd learnt many things in those nine years. The importance of clear, concise, accessible storytelling; the art of précis and crispness in dialogue; and that it's always a good idea to send Deirdre Barlow to prison.

I thought I could put at least two of these lessons, possibly all three if circumstances allowed, to good use as this rover returned to *Doctor Who*.

I think you could say I was slightly miffed not to be on the writing team for that first series back in 2005, but there is no truth in the rumour that I was seen, face pressed to the windows of the BBC Wales production office, dribbling and trailing blood from my fingernails as I scrabbled desperately to be admitted. That would have been completely unprofessional. Anyway I'd got the wrong door. It was the *Pobol y Cwm* production office. Ended up writing that for four years.

I was assured by showrunner Russell T Davies (of *Doctor Who*, not *Pobol y Cwm*) that I was on the writing subs bench, after he had returned, I think having read, my six-part story synopsis for the return of Kroll. I had assumed that maybe the new series was going one of those 'dark reimaginings' for which I would not be suitable as I am afraid of the dark and incapable of imagining things more than once. However, my duties on the *Doctor Who Magazine* comic strip, for which I was to write the Ninth Doctor's first story, meant I was furnished with the shooting scripts for the opening half of Series One.

And what scripts they were.

Barely five pages into *Rose* I could tell this was going to be an enormous popular hit. The scripts were light, they were serious, they were shocking, they were warm. In short, they were *Doctor Who* all over. More *Doctor Who* than *Doctor Who* had ever been.

So I wrote my comic strip (which, with chilling prescience, has the Doctor shouting 'Geronimo!' See, I can do chilling prescience soon as look at you), and shortly thereafter received a praise-packed email from Russell who told me I'd captured Christopher Eccleston's Doctor perfectly. Hot on the heels of this came a message from BBC Books supremo Justin Richards wondering if I'd like to write an original tie-in book to accompany the new series. 'Geronimo!' I cried.

One of the other advantages of my nine-year break was that I had a stock of potential *Doctor Who* stories bubbling away in my mind; one of these even made to TV via the comic strip. The idea that became *Only Human* formed from my fascination with the Neanderthal people after I had read William Golding's heartbreaking novel *The Inheritors* which dealt with their likely extinction at the hands of our ancestors. At the same time I was getting hooked on the books of Steven Pinker, especially *The Blank Slate* which discusses evolutionary psychology – basically why humans are the way we are. For some reason I couldn't get the idea of a Neanderthal adjusting to life in the modern world out of my head. Persistent ideas like that, the ones that just keep nagging away at you, are very rare. And those other naggers, which became *The Lodger* and *Whatever Happened to Sarah Jane?*, have convinced me that persistent voices know what you should be doing, so listen to them. Except the one that nags at you to submit your dark reimagining of *Rentaghost*.

I took a different approach to my previous *Doctor Who* work for the villain of the story, Chantal. My soap experience made we want to nail down her motives and desires and make the character real. So I asked myself what kind of *Doctor Who* villain I would be. What would be my sinister plan? I despair of the Neolithic instincts that formed our brains in the primeval past and still influence and confuse our lives today so unnecessarily. I mean, the fight-or-flight response: very handy on an icy plain when being chased by a woolly mammoth; very irritating in a long queue at the post office. You can't just spear the people in front of you, I've found. So Chantal's desire to improve the human race was an extrapolation of my idle, powerless thoughts, projected onto a much more powerful and slightly more bonkers person than me.

The book became about three very different kinds of human being: the Neanderthals, homo sapiens, and the future humans who had learned to control their emotions and instincts to a dangerous extreme. Set against this were the interlude sequences showing Captain Jack integrating the Neanderthal Das into modern society. Well, into Bromley, which just happened to be where I lived at the time. These turned out to be a lot of people's favourite bits of the book. Despite the fact that they were a sort of desperate improvisation, penned at the last minute when I'd finally worked out what style to write them in. They're diary entries really, not something you could do on TV, but I think they give the book a distinct flavour and a lot of good gags to leaven the horrible things that happen to Rose and the Doctor, like having their heads cut off and getting married.

I am immensely proud of *Only Human*, and very pleased to see it dusted off for the 50th anniversary. I'm also immensely grateful to it. The story I heard was that a copy was left on the desk of Executive Producer Julie Gardner with a post-it note from Russell stuck to the cover, saying 'READ THIS!!!' I can only assume she did, as so many doors opened for me soon after. Within days I was writing *Attack of the Graske*, and not long after that *The Shakespeare Code*, the first of many episodes for *Doctor Who* on the telly.

Over the last 50 years there have been many brilliant *Doctor Who* books. From *An Exciting Adventure With the Daleks* to *Human Nature* to *Shada* (dunno who wrote that). Those books got me reading, got me writing, and got me on the show. I'm so glad that when the series returned so triumphantly in 2005, books were as big a part of it as ever. The last eight years have proved that *Doctor Who*, in some form or other, will be around longer than any of us. And whether or not *Only Human* gets a sentient holographic data-spike reprint for the hundredth anniversary, it's an honour to have contributed even a small part to such a unique literary achievement.

Gareth Roberts
November 2012

For Clayton, as usual,
and for Dad

My Weekend
by Chantal Osterberg (aged 7)
2 October AD 438,533

On Saturday, our cat Dusty was giving the whole family too many wrong-feelings. She weed on the upholstery again. It's nice to have pets to stroke, and we do love Dusty, but she has been too naughty recently. She gets in the way. Later a man over the road tripped over her and broke his leg. That was inconvenient and the man needed a health-patch.

That was when I took a long look at Dusty and decided she was very inefficient. Animals run about for no reason, and they must feel all sorts of odd sensations just like people used to. I thought it would be a good idea to improve Dusty so she would be happier and would understand not to be naughty.

So I went to my room and got out my pen and paper. I had lots of ideas about improvements and I wrote them all down. Then I called Dusty into my room and set to work, using Mother's cutters and things from her work-kit. First I took off her tail, which I consider to be a bit pointless in its present form, so I stretched it

1

and made it scaly. Then I opened Dusty up and moved her organs about to make them more logical. Then I took her head off, pulled her brain out and studied it. It is very primitive, not really what you'd call a brain at all.

I got out one of Mother's gene sprays and dialled it to make Dusty more ferocious at catching mice and better at breeding. I made it so she would never wee again. Then I put all her bits back together and took her downstairs to show to my parents.

Unfortunately, the improved Dusty gave my parents wrong-feelings. They tried to catch her but she sped out of the door and I don't think she'll ever come back.

All the mice are dead now. There was no need for mice, and eventually all cats will be like Dusty because of my cleverness. I like improving things.

So that was my weekend.

Bromley, 2005

The young Roman examined himself in the mirror. He adjusted his purple robe and straightened the circlet of plastic laurel leaves on his head. He was very pleased with himself and how he looked, as usual.

An astronaut walked in behind him, crossed over to the urinal and, with some difficulty, unzipped the flies of his silver space trousers. 'Hey, Dean,' he called over his shoulder to the Roman. 'There's a bloke here really giving Nicola the eye.'

Dean felt a wave of anger rushing up inside him. Which was all right, because he liked feeling angry. Most of his Friday nights ended up like this. It didn't take a lot.

The astronaut finished and did up his flies.

Dean came right up to him. 'What bloke?' he asked. 'The caveman.'

A few moments later, out by the bar, Nicola, who was dressed as a chicken, looked up at Dean through her beak. Oh no, not another scene, not another fight. She shouted to make herself heard over the thudding

3

music. 'Dean, it doesn't matter!'

Dean's mate the astronaut was intent on firing him up. 'He won't leave her alone. Kept eyeing her up while you were in there. I told him she's seeing you…'

Dean looked around the club, over the crowded dance floor. He searched for a caveman among the clowns, schoolgirls, vicars and punks. 'I'm gonna sort it,' he said, feeling the energy crackle through his powerful body. He strode away into the crowd.

Nicola jumped down from her stool and, clutching her golden egg, hopped after him in her three-clawed felt slippers. 'Dean, leave it. It doesn't matter! Dean, not again!'

Dean found the caveman next to the cigarette machine. He was a short-arse, with a dirty black wig and what could have been someone's old carpet wrapped round him. Dean came up behind him, taking long, powerful strides, and tapped him on the shoulder.

'Oi, Captain Caveman!' he shouted. 'You wanna be careful what you're hunting!'

The caveman whipped round, and Dean had a moment to register two things about him: the costume was really good and he stank like a sad old brown pond. Before Dean could notice or do anything else, the caveman let out a terrifying high-pitched wail, bent like an animal and charged him in the middle.

Dean went over backwards, crashing into a table. He heard screams, shouts, the smash of shattering glass. The music stopped mid-thud. Dean sprang back up and launched himself at the caveman, delivering his most powerful punch into his guts. The caveman staggered and then flung himself at Dean, jabbing with his strangely small fists. Dean shielded his face as he was driven back, the world spinning around him. Then he felt his legs kicked out from under him. He was twisted round and forced to his knees, and a muscular, hairy arm locked itself around his neck, squeezing with savage strength.

Dean had the sudden feeling the caveman was going to kill him.

Then the bouncers piled in, three heavy men in bomber jackets pulling the caveman off. Dean sank back, clutching at his throat, gasping for air, the iron tang of blood in his mouth. He looked up. The caveman was struggling with the bouncers, yelping again like a screaming child. He was uncontrollable. Two of the bouncers held him steady, the third smacked him in the jaw. He gave a final squawk and his head sagged forward.

Dean was dragged to his feet by one of the bouncers, his head swimming. 'I didn't start it,' he heard himself protesting. 'He went mental.'

Nicola's face peered at him from inside the chicken's beak. 'That's it! You are chucked!'

Dean pointed feebly at the caveman, who was being dragged to a chair by the bouncers. The lights came on. 'He just went mental,' he repeated.

The astronaut, Tony, stared at the caveman. 'Not him,' he said. 'Him.' He pointed across the club to the mass of startled partygoers on the other side of the dance floor. A puny-looking guy stood there in a torn leopard skin, a comedy dinosaur bone hanging by his side.

Nicola sighed. 'I'm going.' Then she cried out to a friend, 'Cheryl, get us a taxi!' and stalked off.

Dean looked between the two cavemen. He nodded to the one he'd fought. 'Who's that, then?'

Tony shrugged. He looked more closely at the unconscious caveman's face. Under the mop of dirty black hair his bearded features were lumpy, with huge misshapen brows and cheekbones. 'Dunno, but I think Notre-Dame's missing a bell-ringer.'

Dean felt himself being dragged out. Tony tagged along as usual. They headed for the kebab shop. A lot of their Friday nights ended up like this.

It wasn't surprising Tony didn't recognise Dean's opponent. After all, nobody in Bromley had seen a Neanderthal man for 28,000 years.

ONE

'You are gonna love this, Rose,' enthused the Doctor as he leaped from panel to panel of the TARDIS console, his eyes alight with childish optimism in the reflected green glow of the grinding central column.

As always, Rose felt the Doctor's enthusiasm building the same anticipation and excitement in her. She grabbed the edge of the console as the TARDIS gave one of its customary lurches and smiled over at him. 'Tell me more.'

The Doctor spun a dial and threw a lever. 'Kegron Pluva,' he announced grandly.

'OK,' mused Rose. 'That a person or a place? Or some sort of oven spray?'

'Planet.' The Doctor beamed. 'It's got the maddest ecosystem in the universe.' He flung his arms about, demonstrating. 'You've got six moons going one way, three moons going the other way, and a sun that only orbits the planet! Forty-three seasons in one year. The top life form, it's a kind of dog-plant-fungus thing…'

'Top dog-plant-fungus,' laughed Rose.

'Yeah.' The Doctor nodded. 'Plus the water's solid and everyone eats a kind of metal plum…'

Rose held up a hand. 'Enough spoilers. Just let me see it.' She was tingling with pleasure, goosebumps coming up on her arms at the prospect of stepping out from the TARDIS onto this bizarre alien world.

'I'm really gonna regret pointing this out,' said a third voice, 'but… does that mean what I think it means?'

Rose and the Doctor looked up to see Captain Jack, who had joined them in the control room and was pointing to one of the instruments built into the base of the console, a small black box which was emitting a steady flashing red light. He knelt down and fiddled with some buttons on the box.

The Doctor joined him and slapped his hand playfully. 'You're still here, then,' he said, shaking his head mock-ruefully. 'I've gotta remember, put the parental control on.'

Rose looked the captain over. He had obviously been plundering the Doctor's incredibly extensive wardrobe in the depths of the TARDIS and was wearing an old-fashioned Merchant Navy outfit in blue serge with white piping.

'Hello, sailor,' she said, joining him and the Doctor under the console.

Captain Jack smiled. 'I wondered which one of you was gonna say that first.'

Rose winced. 'Could those trousers be any tighter?'

'Is that a request?' he asked with raised eyebrows, before returning his attention to the flashing light. 'So, isn't that a temporal distortion alert?'

The Doctor pressed some buttons on the box and

then he stood up. 'Yeah. I've linked the relay to the screen so we can trace the distortion to its point of origin.'

Rose and the captain stood up and looked over the Doctor's shoulder as he hammered away at the keyboard under the TARDIS's computer screen. A maze of graphics, in the incomprehensible alien script the Doctor always worked in, flickered across it, changing shape every time he pressed the return key.

'Should be able to narrow it down in a bit,' said the Doctor.

'Temporal distortion's a bad thing, then?' Rose surmised. 'I don't suppose it's coming from Kegron Pluva?'

The Doctor performed a final flourish on the keyboard and a row of alien symbols appeared on the screen with a satisfied beep. 'No such luck,' he said dismissively, gesturing to the screen. 'Nobody on Kegron Pluva would be as stupid as...' He left the sentence unfinished, looking slightly awkwardly across at Rose.

Rose recognised the tone of voice the Doctor reserved for dissing humans. 'Oh, right, it's coming from Earth,' she said. 'Interesting year?'

'Let's have a look,' said the Doctor, and rattled at the keyboard again. Another row of symbols appeared. 'Yeah,' he said, intrigued. 'Pretty interesting.'

The captain read the display and turned to Rose. 'Interesting, cos why the hell is someone using a dirty rip engine to travel to your time?'

The Doctor performed another manoeuvre on the

keyboard and got another result. 'To visit Bromley,' he added, mystified. He started adjusting the controls on the console, obviously changing course to the source of the distortion.

Rose shrugged. 'Ah, well. Kegron Pluva, Bromley… probably both about as weird.'

Afternoon sunshine beamed down on Bromley's library gardens. A solitary pensioner sat on a bench dedicated to some long-forgotten council dignitary, scattering crumbs from a paper bag to some excited pigeons and missing his poor dead wife. The regular boom of bass drifted over from the high street, where members of a local evangelical church were hoping to rap the Saturday shoppers into turning to the arms of Jesus. A lost dog sniffed around the flower beds wishing it had some canine company, unaware of the posters put up by its heartbroken owners.

Then, in the far corner of the gardens, between a notice board and a dustbin, there came the rasping and grating sound of ancient unearthly engines. A light began to flash illogically in mid-air. Seconds later, the police box shell of the TARDIS had faded up from transparency. The pigeons scattered, the dog looked over curiously, but the pensioner, who was as good as deaf, didn't notice at all.

Rose was first out of the doors. She looked about and wondered why she wasn't depressed by the familiarity, the utter ordinariness, of the scene. Then she remembered. Nowhere in the universe could be dull when the Doctor was at your side.

'OK, boys,' she called back through the doors. 'Give me the technical stuff. Dirty rip engine?'

The Doctor and Captain Jack emerged. 'Really primitive, nasty way to time travel,' said the Doctor. He nodded to the captain. 'Even worse than his. Rip engines, they just punch a big hole in time. It gets messy.' He frowned for a second, looking round the gardens, and then his face burst out into one of its sudden dazzling smiles. 'I've been here before. Used to be a brass band over there, every Sunday without fail. Everybody came down after church for a stroll. Lots of copping off, in an Edwardian way. You know, going as far as holding hands.'

'Oh yeah?' asked Rose. 'And whose hand were you holding?'

'No one's,' said the Doctor casually.

'Surprise,' Jack commented ironically.

The Doctor bit his lip. 'I can't remember the exact details of what happened that day... but I think nearly everyone survived.'

Rose brought him back to the present. 'And we care about this engine, because...' she prompted.

The captain answered for him. 'They blow up. That's when people say, "Oh, so rip engines are a really primitive, nasty way to time-travel, let's stop using them." If they get the time before they're atomised.'

'We've gotta find whoever's come here and stop 'em using it again to go back,' said the Doctor, striding across the gardens towards the noise of traffic and people from the high street. 'Or it could be "Goodbye, Bromley", "Adios, Beckenham", "Sayonara, Swanley",

"Thank you and goodnight, Orpington".'

Rose and the captain followed him.

'So it isn't the whole universe in danger this time, just the whole of north Kent?'

The Doctor shot her a gently reprimanding look.

'OK, OK, I care,' said Rose.

They turned past the library into the high street. Rose knew the place very vaguely, but it had the usual homogenised look of all the town centres of her time, with the logos of familiar brands stretching up and down the shops on either side of the pedestrianised road. It was packed with shoppers and she could tell it was a Saturday by the numbers of children and teenagers. She saw the captain looking up and down and waited for his verdict.

'So this is the home turf?' he said at last.

'Not really, but near enough.'

A small knot of people about Rose's age passed by and the captain nodded. 'And some of them are as pretty as you.'

The Doctor coughed. 'Er, can we focus?'

'OK,' said Jack. He checked the device he always kept strapped to his wrist. Rose wasn't entirely sure what it could and couldn't do, but it was a useful bit of tech. She watched as he fiddled with the controls and peered at its tiny readout screen.

'I'm picking up vague traces of local distortion,' he said. 'No definite fix. But it happened very recently and very close.'

The Doctor produced the sonic screwdriver from

one of the pockets of his jacket. 'We can use this to narrow the trace down…' He activated it and the tip glowed blue as he swept the screwdriver around.

'Wouldn't someone have noticed?' asked Rose.

'We're time travellers, no one's noticed us,' the Doctor said reasonably.

The captain winked and waved at a couple of girls across the street. 'Speak for yourself.'

The Doctor coughed again. 'Can I have some focus? Even you can't flirt simultaneously with the entire population of a town.' He ran the whirring screwdriver around Jack's wrist device. 'I'll just fine-tune the locator matrix of this thing…' There was a buzzing sound and the Doctor frowned. 'Getting a bit of interference. A lot of people round here have got Sky+.'

Rose was still looking round at the crowd. 'This rip engine going off… Someone must have seen something.'

The Doctor smiled. 'Doubt it. This is your species we're talking about. You didn't notice your planet was spherical for about four million years and when people did you stuck 'em on a bonfire.'

Rose looked across the street and, when she saw a particular shop, a thought occurred to her. 'Are you two gonna be here for a bit fiddling with that?'

'Yeah,' said the Doctor, making another adjustment.

'Right, back in half an hour,' said Rose, and walked off.

Five minutes later she was sitting opposite a

formidable-looking woman, her hand stretched over the counter between them, finding things out. Her mum always picked up any vital and not so vital gossip from places like this, and her simple question, 'What was all that business last night?', had already brought results. There'd been a bigger than normal fight in a local nightclub. Rose had written that off as being the last thing the Doctor would be interested in, but then the woman said something very significant as she tended Rose's nails.

'Looked like a caveman. And of course he only got in cos it was fancy dress. He was like some kind of savage. Homeless, hairy and stank like a dog's blanket. Probably on drugs.'

'You were there?' asked Rose.

The woman finished shaping Rose's nails, ignoring her question. 'Right, I'm just going to give you the basic topcoat. Pearl pink OK?' She started to apply polish.

Rose needed more details. 'So how did the fight start?'

'He just set on the lad.' She nodded over the nail bar at a colleague. 'According to Karen, he virtually trashed the place. They don't know their own strength on drugs. Probably don't even know their own names.' There was a pause as she searched for one of her stock customer conversation pieces. 'Going on holiday soon?'

Rose was thinking about what she'd heard and replied vaguely, 'Well, I was, but something cropped up at work.'

'Sad. Where were you going, then?' Rose found she couldn't make up anything in time – she'd never been a good liar. 'Kegron Pluva,' she muttered.

'Oh, I think Pauline from Gregg's went there last October,' said the woman blithely. 'Got a last-minute deal. Thought it was nice but the hotel was a long way from the beach.'

'So what happened to the caveman?' pressed Rose.

'According to Karen, it took three bouncers to knock him out. Police turned up but he was still out cold, so they called an ambulance.'

Rose considered. 'So they took him to hospital? Which hospital?'

For the first time the woman looked up at Rose, noticing something a little odd about her questions. 'Well, it would have been Southam, I suppose,' she said.

'Right,' said Rose, trying her best to look normal.

There was a pause before the woman asked curiously, 'What do you do for a living, then?'

Rose smiled. 'I used to work in a shop. Then I got something better.'

The Doctor and Captain Jack were still bent over the captain's wrist device when Rose returned. 'There's a trace about six or seven miles north,' the captain was saying. 'Must be the rip engine operator. But that's a pretty wide spread, so it's gonna be tough finding this guy.'

'There's a caveman in Southam Hospital,' said Rose proudly. 'A real caveman by the sound of it.'

The Doctor and the captain stared blankly at her. She waved a freshly painted hand at them. 'I asked over in the nail bar.'

The Doctor looked across at the sign, which read GET NAILED. 'Why didn't I think of that?'

The captain sighed and covered the wrist device with the cuff of his sailor's shirt. 'Back to the TARDIS, then.'

'We could just get the bus,' Rose pointed out as they retraced their steps to the library gardens.

'I don't do buses,' said the Doctor. Suddenly he stopped and looked at Rose. 'Hang on – *caveman?*'

TWO

Weronika pulled back the curtain around the bed, plumped the pillows under the hairy head of its occupant and gave a kindly but professional tut. 'I know you're awake,' she called lightly.

The boy in the bed was pretty ugly even for an Englishman. Weronika had a low opinion of young Englishmen. She reminded herself that this was probably because she spent a lot of her time with the ones who needed patching up after the traditional national pastime of Friday-night pints and fights. The staff at the hospital came from an incredible variety of places – on this ward alone there were Indian, Ukrainian, Polish and Vietnamese nurses – and although English was their common tongue, they shared an unspoken ennui about their charges, the people who had spread it round the world.

'It's time for a bath,' she told the boy, a little louder.

She could see his eyes moving under the heavy lids. His brow was unusually prominent and his lips were thick, dry and cracked. His hair and straggly beard were wild and he smelled... odd. Weronika couldn't place it. Most of the casualty cases reeked of tobacco or drink or stale urine. This one was equally pungent but there was a strange kind of freshness, of outdoorsness, about him.

'Time for a bath,' she repeated, tapping him lightly on the shoulder.

His eyes flicked open, but they didn't contain the usual look of pub-brawl aftermath – amusement or regret. Weronika took a step back. The boy's eyes were a vivid sea green, with unusually large and dark pupils. And they were filled with sheer, animal terror.

'You're going to be fine,' she told him. 'All you need is to freshen up and you'll be home by lunchtime.' She realised he wasn't getting a word. He wasn't English. 'What is your name?' she asked slowly and clearly.

He didn't answer. She realised his entire body was clenched tight. She smiled broadly and gave him a reassuring stroke. To her relief, he slowly raised his hand from beneath the bedclothes and gently took hers. He'd been dressed in a gown the night before and the dazzling white crispness of the garment made an unusual contrast with his hairy forearm. Weronika stared at his arm. It wasn't just hairy; it was bordering on *furry*.

Gently she guided him to sit up, then led him by the hand down the ward to the bathroom. He walked slowly and hesitantly, never taking his eyes off her. With a sudden stab of pity, Weronika wondered if the blow to his head had been more severe than A&E had thought last night, or if there'd been something wrong before. There'd been no identification on him and no friends or family had come looking for him. She'd need to speak to Sister, right after the bath.

They entered the bathroom and Weronika let go of his hand and twisted the taps. The boy stared at them, mesmerised, as if he'd never seen running water before. Weronika gestured to him to remove his gown. He stared back at her blankly. Still smiling, she reached behind him and undid the ties. He seemed glad to get out of the gown, lifting his heavy arms for her to pull it off.

The first thing Weronika noticed about his naked body was that it was covered in coarse, thick hair. The second thing she noticed was that his body went straight from stomach to groin.

He bent over the bath and eagerly scooped up handfuls of water, drinking it down with enormous gulps.

That was when Weronika decided she'd better talk to Sister straight away. She'd seen plenty of English people naked before and they'd all had waists.

'With any luck they'll not have noticed anything weird yet,' the Doctor told Jack, tapping his fingers on the edge of the TARDIS console as it flew through the vortex to the hospital. One eye was on the coordinate settings, one was on a copy of the A–Z of London in his other hand. This materialisation had to be a particularly precise one. 'But we've still gotta move on this rescue quick, in case there's anything to notice, and in case they notice it.'

'Then find out what a "caveman" is doing with a rip engine,' said Jack. 'Those things were big in the forty-sixth century. No cavemen then.'

'Yeah, I know that,' said the Doctor patiently. 'You don't have to spell it out for me. I've got a list of questions for him as long as your arm.'

Rose emerged from the inner depths of the TARDIS, prepared to take her part in the Doctor's hastily conceived rescue operation. After a bit of searching she'd found the nurse's outfit on one of the rails at the very back of the TARDIS's enormous wardrobe, between a 1980s ra-ra skirt and an enormous 1780s Venetian ball gown. She walked right up to Captain Jack and pulled a challenging face, daring him to make one of his jokes.

Jack pulled an innocent face and held up his hands, though he couldn't help looking Rose's nurse's outfit over from top to toe. 'I'm not saying anything,' he said. 'Look at me not saying anything.'

Rose moved to the Doctor's side. 'If he is some sort of caveman, a savage or whatever, perhaps he hasn't brought the engine with him. He just got beamed back in time or something. In which case, no big danger.'

The Doctor adjusted some of the controls, bringing the TARDIS in to land. 'He sets on someone with his bare hands. Sounds like he's terrified and alone. That's a good enough reason to help someone.' He squinted at the A–Z and spun a lever, and the engines groaned. The floor shuddered under Rose and she felt the particular lurch in the stomach that meant the TARDIS was about to land. 'But the hospital, they'll just think he's a drunk,' the Doctor went on. 'All we need to do is get in, get him and get out. Should be a doddle.'

The TARDIS settled with a satisfying thump.

The Doctor checked the scanner, grinned, gave himself a thumbs-up and dropped the A–Z on the console. Then he strode confidently down the ramp and through the police box doors of the TARDIS, with Rose and the captain following.

The Doctor's precision-navigation had been brilliant, Rose had to admit. He'd materialised the TARDIS over the street, right opposite the hospital. Unfortunately the hospital was surrounded by a line of army vans. Some of the armed soldiers were taking up positions at the doors of the various departments. A steady stream of staff and patients was emerging from the main reception area, being hustled along by officers to join the crowds sealed off behind yellow lines of incident tape at either end of the street. There was a steady crackle of radio communications. A black helicopter buzzed overhead.

Rose turned to the Doctor, who was trying his best not to lose his confident smile. 'Or it could be really, really difficult,' he said, only slightly less confidently.

Jack frowned. 'Why all this? Sure, he's maybe covered in fleas, but he's just another human.'

'Unless he isn't,' said Rose.

'Slight change of plan,' said the Doctor. He turned to Jack. 'Rose and I are gonna need a distraction. Got one?'

Jack thought for a second and nodded. 'Oh yeah, I've got a distraction. Never fails. One of the biggest distractions you'll ever see.'

'Great,' said the Doctor. He then turned to Rose

and she followed him as he crossed the road to the hospital. He shouted back over his shoulder to Jack, 'Give us five minutes – and distract!'

A few moments later, the Doctor and Rose had pushed through the confused crowd at the main doors and were walking through reception. The scene was one of utter confusion, as patients and staff were being bundled from descending lifts by soldiers with rifles slung across their shoulders.

'Don't worry,' the Doctor told Rose breezily as they walked towards the large flight of stairs at the far end of the reception area. 'Just do that thing like you own the place.'

'I do own it, it's the NHS,' observed Rose.

People were hurrying by without giving her a second glance.

'See,' said the Doctor. 'You stick on the right gear, they think you belong here.'

Rose smiled, looking up and down at his leather jacket and jeans. 'How do you get away with it, then?'

'I belong everywhere,' said the Doctor. And as if to prove his point he collared a woman in a cleaner's uniform, who was half walking, half running in the opposite direction. 'Hello, what's all this about, then?'

Rose wasn't surprised when the woman immediately stopped and smiled back at the Doctor. How did he do that?

'They're isolating the place,' the woman said, eyes alight with the guilty thrill of breaking bad news. 'Brought in this feller last night, turns out he's got the

Ebola virus!' She started moving again, brushing by them. 'We've all gotta clear out!'

'Well, that's what they're telling her,' the Doctor said.

'What if it's true? It would explain all the panic,' Rose pointed out.

The Doctor shook his head. 'Nah, impossible. It's the first rubbish panicky lie they'd think of. If there's any risk of infection they'd be keeping people in, not sending 'em out. Plus, Ebola jumps to humans in 1976, gets cured in 2076. No time-travel tech in that century.'

Rose smiled again. 'Don't you ever get tired, knowing everything?' she asked teasingly.

By now they'd reached the staircase. Just as they were about to start up it, a soldier blocked their path, pointing to the main doors. 'You have to move out! Please!' he shouted.

The Doctor and Rose turned on their heels and started back the other way. Rose flicked a glance at her watch. 'Where's that distraction?'

Suddenly there was a commotion up ahead at the main doors. There were shrieks and, strangely, a few howls of what sounded to Rose like embarrassed laughter. For a moment she couldn't see what was going on. Then Captain Jack burst through the crowd, whooping wildly, totally naked.

Rose turned her head away automatically, before risking a peek back. Jack was now sprinting for one of the lifts, just as the door was closing. The soldier on duty at the staircase ran to stop him, joining the general scramble through the stunned crowd.

Rose looked at the floor. 'For shame,' she muttered, though she couldn't help smiling at the captain's nerve.

The Doctor gave a hoot of laughter. 'Nah, that's not the biggest distraction I've ever seen.' Then he grabbed Rose's arm, shouting, 'Come on! Run!'

They raced up the now unguarded stairs three at a time.

It was surprisingly easy to find what they were looking for. The corridors of the hospital were all but abandoned and the Doctor soon found a wall map of the building that marked the isolation rooms on the seventh floor.

They reached the seventh floor – Rose gasping a bit from the exertion of pelting up fourteen flights of stairs, the Doctor not even slightly out of breath – and made their way down a long, echoing corridor. Voices were coming from the far end. They crept along and came to a room with a large window onto the corridor. Carefully they knelt down and popped their heads over the sill.

Rose saw a small group of white-coated doctors standing round a patient. There was also a kind-looking young female nurse standing at one side, observing the scene with concern, and a puzzled-looking army officer. Rose stared more closely at the white-gowned patient. He was short, and her first thought was that he was a child, or perhaps in his early teens. Then one of the doctors moved to one side and she saw his face. His features were heavy: he had an enormous nose, seemingly flattened out at the edges, a huge lumpy brow and thick bushy eyebrows. Somehow, although everything was there, his features didn't add up to the totally human package.

'Not a human, then?' she whispered.

The Doctor grunted. 'Depends on your definition. Definitely not an alien.'

Memories of half-forgotten science lessons and half watched BBC2 documentaries filtered through Rose's mind. She found the word she was looking for. 'He's a Neanderthal. They died out millions of years ago.'

'About 28,000 years ago,' the Doctor corrected casually. 'In evolutionary terms, last Tuesday.'

Rose frowned. 'And they had rip engines, time travel?' She doubted that but was quite prepared for the Doctor to prove her wrong.

He shook his head. 'Nah. They were clever all right, but not that clever.' He pulled a puzzled face, then shrugged and smiled. 'We'll work that out later.'

'Suppose you know loads of Neanderthals,' teased Rose.

'Met a couple, yeah.' He looked right at her, his face clouding over with a hint of disquiet. 'And it wasn't so much they died out as they were weakened. The climate changed and they couldn't compete.'

Rose quickly got up to speed with what was troubling him. 'With humans? Humans finished them off?'

The Doctor nodded. 'And they might do it again if we don't get him out of there.'

Rose looked back through the window. The Neanderthal man's face was frozen in a kind of silent fear. He was plainly terrified of the people round him. She turned to the Doctor again.

'I'm human,' she reminded him. 'We're not all the same.'

The Doctor smiled. 'Yeah, you do get nice ones. Now and again.'

Weronika considered her English to be fairly good, but she was finding it hard to keep up with the hushed conversation among these doctors, none of whom belonged to the hospital, and military men. She'd reported the patient's unusual qualities to Sister, who'd referred it to one of their doctors, who'd taken some photos and X-rays and emailed them off somewhere. About twenty minutes later the order came through to evacuate and all these strangers had turned up. Weronika had hung around the patient and nobody had bothered to dismiss her. She guessed she just wasn't important enough. None of the new arrivals had taken any interest in her either. Their attention was fixed on the patient. They kept looking at him, shaking their heads and muttering a word she didn't recognise. Neanderthal.

She'd sedated the boy and watched the immobile terror fade from his eyes. Now she stood back, fearing for him. Something told Weronika that whatever he was, and whatever these strangers decided, it would not be good for him. She had a feeling of powerlessness. She wanted to shoo them all out and simply care for him, but she didn't dare.

Suddenly the door of the isolation ward burst open and a man dressed in leather jacket and jeans, with severely cropped hair and eyes that blazed with blue fire, and a startlingly pretty young female nurse burst in. Just as Weronika had distrusted the other strangers she felt an immediate liking and trust for these two; it was as if a subconscious signal somewhere in the back of her mind had been tripped. She just knew they were good people.

'Hello,' said the man confidently. 'Sorry I'm late. I'm Dr…' His eyes swivelled round the room and lit on the bedside table. 'I'm Dr Table. I'm the country's leading expert in severe acromegaly, and just by taking one look at that man I can see that he needs my help, and if you're thinking he's some kind of Neanderthal throwback you are so wrong, but it's an easy mistake to make and I won't hold it against you, so if you'll just hand him over to me I'll get it sorted out and give him the best possible care and attention.' The words rushed out of him in a tone that was warm, casual and authoritative all at the same time. Before anybody could get a word in, he started to speak to the nurse who was with him. 'Nurse Tyler –' he turned to Weronika and grinned, and it felt like the sun emerging from behind black clouds – 'and you, please put him on a trolley.'

Weronika found herself obeying as if it was the most natural thing in the world.

As she and the other nurse lifted the boy onto a trolley, she heard one of the doctors give a sigh of relief that was almost pained. 'Acromegaly,' he said. 'Of course.'

'Yeah,' said the stranger, 'it's a tragic debilitating condition and I, Dr Table, am the greatest expert in treating it. So you can just call off all these silly soldiers and let me help this man. I've got an ambulance parked outside, so…'

By this time he was already following Weronika, Nurse Tyler and the trolley out into the corridor and towards the lift.

'See?' he said brightly, addressing Nurse Tyler. 'Told ya. So relieved when someone comes in with an answer and sets their minds at rest. Doddle.' He shot a glance over at Weronika and read her name badge. 'Hello, Weronika. How's Krakow? Haven't been to Wawel since I slew that dragon, about thirteen hundred years ago.'

Weronika found herself smiling back.

As they entered the lift, she found herself wanting to scream, *I don't know who you are, but take me with you!* She looked over at Nurse Tyler and thought, *If you're his friend – I wish I was you.*

He pressed the button for the ground floor and the doors closed. Then he took the hand of the boy on the trolley. 'You're gonna be all right, mate. I'm the Doctor. And I'm not one of Them. I look like one, but I'm not, OK?'

To Weronika's astonishment the boy looked right back at him and said, in a high girlish voice that she hadn't expected at all, 'OK.'

'Come on, come on,' said Nurse Tyler, thumbing the

lift button again.

An alarm started ringing. The Doctor's face fell.

'I know it's wrong of me,' said Nurse Tyler, grinning at the Doctor, 'but I'm actually pleased that didn't work.'

Weronika pushed open the lift doors and started pulling the trolley out and round a corner. She could hear urgent running footsteps under the alarm.

'This way,' she called back to them. 'The service lift!'

The Doctor caught up with her and gave her another of his devastating smiles. 'Two nice humans!' he cried inexplicably.

Weronika's heart fluttered with excitement. She felt she had never been more alive.

They helped her drag the trolley into the service lift.

The doors of the service lift opened onto the draughty, empty corridor leading up to the kitchens. A back door was covered by a large metal grille. Weronika leaped ahead and pulled it open with one mighty heave, and the others pushed the trolley out into the forecourt that gave onto a back street. The alarms were still clanging away and Nurse Tyler had to shout to make herself heard. When she did, she used another word Weronika had never heard before. 'The TARDIS is round the front!'

Booted feet were rushing towards them across the tarmac. The soldiers were running round and would be on them at any moment. The Doctor clicked his fingers, looking about for inspiration. 'We need another distraction.'

Nurse Tyler bit her lip. 'No way!'

'It doesn't have to be that kind of distraction,' said the Doctor. He turned to Weronika and pointed to the right, in the direction of the oncoming soldiers. 'Weronika, you're a good woman, lie to them!'

Then he grabbed the trolley and set off around the left side of the building at an incredible speed, with Nurse Tyler following.

Weronika knew she had only seconds left with these strange, wonderful people. 'Who are you?' she called after them desperately.

'You'll never know!' the Doctor shouted back, without turning. 'But you've helped me save a life! That's a good day's work in your job!'

And with that he was gone around a corner – a second before the soldiers arrived in the forecourt.

Weronika pointed back through the doors into the hospital corridor. 'They've gone inside again!' she shouted.

The soldiers pushed past her and swarmed into the building.

Weronika sagged against the wall. She felt that her life was never going to be as exciting again.

Fortunately the soldiers had all run round to the back of the building, summoned by the alarm. The Doctor and Rose sped across the road before anybody in the crowd of startled onlookers could stop them.

The trolley slammed into the police box doors of the TARDIS. The Doctor already had the key in the lock and was hustling the Neanderthal to his feet. He bundled him inside and made to follow.

Rose grabbed his shoulder. 'What about Jack?'

They heard a wild whooping as the naked Jack ran towards them across the road. Rose looked away.

'Distracting enough?' he asked as he joined them.

'Please just put something on!' cried Rose as they entered the TARDIS.

Rose led the Neanderthal, who seemed no more dazed by the cavernous interior of the TARDIS than anything else, to a chair. Jack had slipped off into the interior to find some more clothes, while the Doctor was over by the console, rocking on his heels and using the scanner function of the computer screen to view the milling crowd outside, trying unsuccessfully to stifle his mirth at the confusion he'd caused.

Rose coughed and pointed to their guest. 'Shall I make him a cup of tea or something?'

'We don't wanna frighten him any more,' said the Doctor, coming over. 'You never stew the bag. Whip it in, whip it out, that's you.' He knelt down and smiled at the Neanderthal. 'He's been sedated but that'll wear off.'

'He looks terrified,' said Rose.

The Doctor was suddenly serious. 'Culture shock. Stranded in a world where nothing makes sense. We've gotta get him back home as soon as possible.'

Rose whispered to the Doctor, 'Now he's in the TARDIS, can he understand us? Can he talk?'

She was referring to a property of the TARDIS that entered the minds of its occupants, changing them so they could understand any language, spoken or written, as if it was their own.

'Of course I can talk,' said the Neanderthal.

Rose jumped. His voice was very loud and high-pitched, almost like a parrot's.

'Sorry,' she said. She held out her hand to him and smiled. 'I'm Rose. What are you called?'

'Das,' he said. He stared at her, his eyes narrowing. Then he said very slowly, 'This is the future, isn't it? A time to come.'

'Yeah,' said Rose. She turned to the Doctor. 'How'd he work that out?'

'You think I'm stupid,' Das went on. 'Your lot always think we're stupid. This must be the future. And it's full of your people. So where are my people?'

The Doctor shared an uncomfortable look with Rose. He smiled at Das, but for him it wasn't very convincing. 'You're going home, pal. That's all that matters.'

Captain Jack returned to the control room, this time wearing a tight-fitting pair of black plastic trousers and a white T-shirt cut off at the arms.

Rose rolled her eyes. 'It's a Village Person.'

'I can take it all off again if you like.' He then became serious, holding up his wrist device and pressing a button. A cone of light shone up from it, filled with a dizzying array of algebraic symbols and a tiny hologram of Earth. 'I've reverse-traced the distortion from the rip engine. We should end up right back where he started from.'

'Which is when?' asked Rose.

'Just when you'd think,' replied Jack. 'He left Bromley on Wednesday 24 May in the year 29,185 BC. And shouldn't we be asking him how?'

Das took the lead from Jack. 'I was following Reddy, one of your people. He kept coming to the forest, bringing strange made-things. Like that, kind of.' He pointed to Jack's wrist device. 'Ka said he was from the future. He went to a strange tree. He opened it and I followed him inside. To a strange cave, full of made-things. Then suddenly I was in this world.'

Jack sighed. 'Time travellers with a dirty rip engine at one of the most delicate points of human history. That's insane.'

Rose smiled at him. 'So you mucking about in time is OK, but anyone else is irresponsible and mental?'

'I knew what I was doing,' said Jack defensively.

Rose recalled their first encounter with Jack in 1940s London and couldn't help saying, 'Yeah, you who almost destroyed the human race by accident.' But she was much more interested in Das. She couldn't quite get her head round the lucid way he had spoken. 'Chatty, isn't he?' she whispered to the Doctor as he returned to the console and started punching up the coordinates for their journey. 'He's coping pretty well.'

'You coped pretty well in the year five billion,' he reminded her. 'Much bigger gap. And he's practically one of the family.'

'I want to go back, but I must know about the future,' said Das. 'Where are my people?'

'I can't answer your questions,' the Doctor called over. 'You're going back home. Just try and forget today. It was only a mad, bad dream.'

Das stood up. 'We're going back to the forest? You can do that?'

'Yeah,' said the Doctor. 'I promise. Easy as pie.'

With that, he tugged the lever that operated the engines, and gave a smirk and a wave at the crowd on the scanner screen as the TARDIS dematerialised. Then he looked at his watch, checked a dial on the console and said, 'Should be there in about ten minutes, Das.'

The green column at the centre of the console began to rise and fall with its customary wheezing sound. The floor juddered under them. Rose took the opportunity of the general din of take-off to lean close in to the Doctor and whisper, 'We killed them? Humans wiped them out? That's what you said. But he's… just like us.'

'So if he wasn't, it'd be all right?' said the Doctor evasively.

'You know what I mean, Doctor.' Rose shuddered. 'That's disgusting.'

Before the Doctor could answer, Jack cried, 'Hey!'

The Doctor and Rose whipped round from the console. Das had fallen to the shaking floor of the TARDIS. At first Rose thought he had merely been knocked off his feet by the turbulence of the dematerialisation. Then she saw that he was bathed in an eerie green light…

… and that he was dissolving.

THREE

The Doctor leaped onto the TARDIS console, flattening himself across it and jabbing at a panel on the opposite side. 'No, reverse, reverse!' he shouted. 'No...' He shot an anguished glance over at Das and then pressed about seventeen buttons at once, using fingers, feet, whatever he could. If Rose hadn't been so anxious she would have clapped at that.

The TARDIS gave an almighty shudder – even by its normal standards, Rose thought, as she was first flung to the floor and then back to her feet and waltzered the other way, that was *volcanic*. She heard the joints of her knees and elbows crack. Then she grabbed the rail and held on as the huge, ancient machinery somewhere deep in the bowels of the TARDIS shrieked in agony. She saw something black and white whizz past her and realised it was Jack. The TARDIS gave one last resentful wail, as if it was shouting at the Doctor, *How dare you do this to me!* and then the column settled with a deep percussive rumble.

Rose lifted her head, brushed the hair out of her eyes and let herself drop to the floor. She looked over at the spread-eagled, white-gowned figure of Das. He was out cold, but the eerie glow had faded and he was back to solid reality once again.

She gazed up to see the Doctor stroking the console. 'I am so sorry,' he whispered to it soothingly.

'Don't I get a bit of attention?' she said, hauling herself up by the rail.

The Doctor leaped down from the console and stroked her arm. 'You're gonna be all right,' he said in the same cooing tone of voice.

Rose pulled her arm away. 'No. Save it for your dashboard.'

'I'll have a bit if there's any going,' called Jack. He did a cartwheel and sat up smiling. 'Crash test training. A perfect fall.'

'Then you don't need it,' said Rose. She nodded to Das. 'So what happened there?'

'It's the time distortion,' said the Doctor gravely. 'I used the fast return. We're back in Bromley, the library gardens.'

Jack picked Das up gently and lowered him back into his chair, which was thankfully bolted to the floor. 'The rip engine must have polluted every cell in his body. He can't time-travel again, poor guy, or the vortex pressures will just tear him apart.'

Rose felt a pang of concern. 'What, he can't go home?'

The Doctor didn't reply.

'There's gotta be a way round it,' continued Rose. 'Bring out some of your gadgets. Can't the sonic screwdriver do something?'

The Doctor stood over Das and looked down at him

sadly. Rose noticed he was deliberately not catching her eye. 'No gadgets for this. His cellular structure's been flipped like any time traveller's, like yours or mine, but without the protection we get from the TARDIS – or anything like it.'

'If we try to move him, he'll disintegrate,' said Jack.

'So? We don't need to travel in time. Let's just take him to another planet,' suggested Rose.

'Any journey in the TARDIS causes time ripples,' said the Doctor. 'I can't. And just out of interest, which planet would you suggest?'

Rose knew that little sparks of rudeness like that were just a cover for when something had upset or was worrying him. He was looking anywhere but at her, or at Das. 'So he's stuck here on Earth, in this time, for ever?' she asked. She put herself directly in front of the Doctor, forcing him to look at her. 'What have you promised, Doctor?'

The Doctor caught her eye at last, and just for a moment she saw something that looked small and helpless in there.

Then he snapped back to life, heading for a storage locker built into one of the walls. 'We've gotta go back, Rose, find out how he got here. It doesn't change that.'

Rose trailed him. 'Hang on. He's gonna have to stay here, live here? What are you gonna say to him?'

The Doctor opened the locker and started rooting in it. 'Well, I'm gonna have a lot to sort out,' he said after a while.

Rose sighed. 'So it's me that's gotta tell him.'

'You're a closer relation,' said the Doctor without looking up.

'Half an hour ago you said he was frightened and alone. Now you expect him to live in twenty-first-century Bromley like that was nothing.'

'Well, it's only slightly less primitive.'

Rose walked away. 'Thanks for the joke. Guess what? It's solved everything.'

Jack was standing by Das. 'It isn't the Doctor's fault,' he reminded Rose.

'Yeah, but…' Rose looked down at Das's heavy features and thick eyebrows. 'How can he live here? He's gonna stick out just a bit. Unless he joins Oasis.'

'I don't see we've got any choice,' said Jack.

The Doctor walked over. 'Whoever sent him here, Rose, it's their fault. We've gotta get back and stop 'em doing it again, or doing something worse. They could do such damage.'

She saw that he'd found what he was searching for in the locker. It looked like a credit card. She blinked – it *was* a credit card.

'You three – wait here.' The Doctor was down the ramp and out through the police box doors before Rose could object.

She heard a groan and turned to see Das's eyes flickering open. They settled on her. 'Rose?' he asked.

Rose took his hand. She looked at Jack for support. He just shrugged. Rose pulled a face of ironic thanks at him. Then she swallowed, licked her lips and turned back to Das. 'Listen, there's a problem. A big problem.'

*

It was early evening. The sun, which seemed to comfort Das, was making a twilight showing through the clouds over Bromley and now he sat on a bench in the park, dressed in a jacket and jeans from the TARDIS's wardrobe, with Rose.

Rose found it hard to tell how Das had taken the news that he was trapped in this future for ever. He hadn't cried, or screamed, or run about shouting. Most likely, she came to realise, he simply hadn't believed the Doctor's promise to take him home in the first place.

He looked around the people in the park, taking a particular interest in two things: the pushchairs carrying tiny children and the motor scooters carrying old people. 'This place is full of made-things,' he said. 'You are always making things. All you need are spears, and tools to make spears. That's all anybody really needs. Why do you keep making other things? Making caves, making clothes. Why bother?' He laughed to himself. 'You make things because you're lazy. Here you're too lazy even to walk. Last night I saw fast walking-things.'

'Cars,' guessed Rose.

A plane chose that moment to pass overhead. Rose kept expecting Das to freak out at these sights, but instead he just pointed up and observed, 'And those aren't birds. A flying made-thing?'

'Planes,' said Rose.

Jack walked over from the TARDIS, where he'd been locking in the coordinates for the journey back to Das's time, and picked up the last couple of sentences.

He looked Das full in the eye and said slowly and distinctly, as if to an idiot, 'The planes are machines. For people to fly in. They are not beasts. They were made by people.'

Das blinked at him a little resentfully. 'Yes, I know,' he said patiently. He glanced at Rose and nodded to Jack. 'Is there something wrong with him?'

'He's just a bit slow.' She smiled at Jack. 'He gets it. I've been to the future and I can work things out, so why can't he?'

Jack frowned. 'You're from a level-two technology. You already have a start. You've got concepts of science.'

'And eyes,' said Rose.

Das got up and looked round. 'I am getting it, yes, most of it. But where is the quarry?'

Rose was confused. 'Sorry?'

'Your food. Where are the animals?' A dog came sniffing round the flower beds. 'Ah, you eat dogs. That can't be very filling.'

'We don't need to hunt,' said Rose. 'We get our food from the shops.'

Das frowned. 'The shops?'

'We pay for food in the shops.'

'Pay?'

'With money.'

'Money?'

Jack smirked over at Rose. 'Warned you. You've got some big-time educating to do.'

She had no time to reply because at that moment the Doctor strode up.

'Right, I've sorted a few things out.' He clapped Das on the shoulder. 'How are you?'

'I've got most of it,' he said. 'I'm not clear about food, shops and money.'

'Jack'll explain,' said Rose. She turned to the Doctor. 'We can't simply leave him. He can just about pass for human, but we've got a responsibility.'

'Who said anything about leaving him? He needs a helping hand to get him settled.'

'That's gonna take some time,' said Jack.

'Yeah, it could,' said the Doctor. 'So you'd better get started right away.'

Jack blinked in surprise. 'Me?'

The Doctor took a large envelope from one of his pockets and handed it to Jack. 'All in there. Keys to your flat.' He handed him a piece of paper. 'There's the address.' He pointed. 'Just over thataway. It's a bit poky, and the furniture's disgusting, and the curtains in the front room are falling to bits, and I'd descale the shower head right now if I was you. But it'll do for two young professionals. Ever such a nice estate agent. You'll fancy her, and she's very easily pleased. Oh, and you'd better have this.' He handed Jack the credit card. 'You've got half a million sterling in there. Your pin number is 1. Don't spend it all at once. Come on, Rose.'

Captain Jack looked down, dazed, at the credit card. 'This is a psychic credit card. They were banned after the infinite recession on Baydafarn. I've been trying to get hold of one of these for years...'

'And now you've got one,' said the Doctor, leading

Rose to the TARDIS. 'Back in a month! Four weeks exactly.'

Rose stopped off to address Das. 'Das, the captain's gonna look after you, get you up on your feet here… It'll be OK. It's fine. Most of the people are really nice.'

'Get him some decent clothes,' said the Doctor, unlocking the TARDIS doors. 'They've got a good Gap in Croydon. Works for me. See ya.'

Jack hurried up to them. 'Doctor, I don't belong here.'

'That's all right,' said the Doctor, nodding to Das. 'Neither does he, yet.'

'And you can blend in anywhere,' said Rose teasingly. 'You're the boy who says he's seen and done it all.'

'Isn't Rose a better choice for this?' protested Jack. 'She's from this time, she knows the area. Wouldn't I be more use to you where you're going?'

The Doctor hesitated a second. 'Maybe, but I like Rose.' And as Rose stepped inside the TARDIS, he called back, 'Stay out of trouble, handsome! And keep your hand on your ha'penny!'

Jack stood back as the TARDIS disappeared with its usual rasping and grating noise. Das barely flinched; Jack guessed he'd seen so many things that were strange to him today that one more didn't make much difference. And nobody else in the park had noticed at all.

Jack looked round. So he had a month to settle a Neanderthal man in twenty-first-century London. He felt a little left out – but on the other hand it was a challenge. It might even be fun. He clapped a hand round Das's shoulder and asked, 'Shall we learn about shops, then?'

FOUR

The sun rose over the country that was later to be known as Britain on Thursday 25 May 26,185 BC. Somewhere under the area that would later be known as Bromley on that day, a man called Jacob was tucking into his breakfast of cauliflower cheese. He realised he wasn't enjoying it very much, so he reached for the small, brightly coloured metal pack attached to his breast and tapped in a five-digit combination on its small keyboard without looking. Then the breakfast of cauliflower cheese became incredibly tasty, one of the best meals he'd ever had. But then, most of his meals tasted like the best meal he'd ever had. So he punched another five-digit combination into the metal pack and then the cauliflower cheese tasted like nothing he'd ever tasted before, in a strange but very pleasant way.

He heard his wife, Lene, enter the living room of their married quarters. She gave a little sigh as she pulled her chair up to the breakfast bar and poured herself some cauliflower cheese juice.

'What's the matter, darling?' asked Jacob.

She didn't say anything, just stared into space with an expression he didn't recognise.

'Lene?'

'You know I took that diagnostic test yesterday?' said Lene casually. 'The result's just come through from Chantal, on my phone.' She still had her phone in her hand. She flipped it open and stared at the little screen.

Jacob felt a pang of wrong-feeling about her expression. He found he wanted to know – desperately wanted to know – what the result was. That felt uncomfortable. 'What is it?'

'Incipient renal collapse,' said Lene.

Jacob felt the wrong-feeling swell inside him. 'How long have you got?' he asked.

'Three weeks at the outside,' said Lene. 'It's no surprise, I guess. I am 387 and no one can live for ever.' She smiled, but it wasn't a proper, fine smile.

Jacob didn't know quite how to feel.

'Where's my popper pack?' asked Lene. 'I put it down somewhere last night…'

Jacob found her pack under a cushion on their settee and quickly handed it over. Lene took it and pressed its soft, adhesive pad to her chest.

'Right, quickly…' said Jacob. He opened the kitchen drawer and fished out the instruction booklet. He scanned through it, searching the index. 'Bad news, bad news… page 43.' He turned to it. 'Ah. Here we go. "News of your impending termination… Combo 490/32".'

'490/32,' Lene repeated, tapping the numbers into her pack. Immediately the wrong smile and the strange expression disappeared.

'And I'll need "News of partner's impending termination",' said Jacob, searching for it among the lines of crabbed text. '"Combo 490/37".'

He tapped the code into his pack and the wrong-feelings disappeared. He smiled at Lene and took her hand.

'It's a shame, isn't it?' he said.

'Can't be helped,' Lene smiled back. 'And we had ninety fantastic years together.'

A buzzer sounded. Jacob looked at the large wall-clock, which told him it was just gone nine. 'I'm late for work. I'll see you later.'

He grabbed his briefcase, took one last bite of cauliflower cheese and hurried out.

'Bye, Jacob, see you later,' called Lene.

After he'd gone she drank her cauliflower cheese juice. It tasted a bit ordinary, so she tapped a code into her popper pack and then it tasted like cheesecake, her favourite flavour. Then she yawned and stretched and drew the curtains, and spotted a stain on the carpet. Damn! Just after she'd tidied up, and Jacob had done his typical irritating thing of leaving a drink balanced on the arm of the settee!

She tapped another code into her pack to stop the stain and Jacob's carelessness annoying her, and went and got out the spray from under the sink.

'Afternoon, Jacob,' said Chantal, pointedly but warmly, as he hurried into the control area.

'Sorry, sorry…' said Jacob, slipping behind his desk.

'And today's excuse is?' asked Chantal.

Jacob bit his lip. 'Well, you know Lene's been feeling… oh, what's the word?'

'Content?' guessed Chantal.

'No,' said Jacob, struggling. 'It means… body not working properly… begins with s, I think…'

'Serene?'

Jacob clicked his fingers, retrieving the right word. 'Sick. That's the one. She's been feeling sick. Turns out it's an impending termination, renal collapse.'

Chantal's face fell in that strange way. 'Yes, I know. I examined her myself.'

'It's 490/35,' said Jacob helpfully.

Chantal tapped it in. 'Thanks.' She smiled. 'OK, Jacob, no worries, darling. Can you cover the East Sector Sweep climate reports for me today?' She walked over and put down a sheaf of papers on his desk.

Jacob nodded. 'Fine.'

'You're a star.'

He started to leaf through the reports. He remembered there was a question he needed to ask. Thinking about the question gave him a wrong-feeling, which was easily dealt with, but still the question remained. 'Er, Chantal…'

'Yes, Jacob?'

'When are we going home?'

'Not for a bit yet. Do you want to go home?'

Jacob wrestled with the words. 'I… find myself… thinking about it. And I keep thinking about Pedro and Suzy. Where are they?'

'They're around,' said Chantal.

'They went down to the Grey Door and I haven't seen them since,' said Jacob slowly. 'I haven't seen Maria either.'

'They're around,' repeated Chantal. 'Somewhere.' She came over and gave him a comforting hug. 'Oh, Jacob, you total berk. You should have said. You're anxious.'

'A little,' Jacob admitted.

'354/91's best for that,' advised Chantal, kissing him on the forehead.

'Oh, thanks,' said Jacob.

'No probs,' said Chantal.

Jacob tapped the code in and relaxed. The anxious wrong-feeling evaporated. Jacob was aware that he still didn't have the answer to his question, and he was sure that Pedro, Maria and Suzy weren't around anywhere either, but it didn't seem to matter much any longer, so he got back to studying the climate reports.

His wife was dying and he was trapped in primeval history, but what the hell.

Rose felt a surge of excitement as the engines quietened down and the TARDIS settled. This was always the best bit for her. Through those doors there was another world, another time!

At first she'd wondered if she'd get used to it one day, turn into a seasoned traveller, hard to impress. But she saw the same look of glee on the Doctor's face every time and he'd been doing it for 900 years. So it was one of those exciting things you never got used to and that sometimes made her feel so good she wanted to scream it out.

She pushed open the door and stepped outside. The comforting warmth of the TARDIS was replaced by a biting wind that stung her cheeks. The air was the freshest she'd tasted, and she felt the urge to run out and take down great lungfuls of it.

They'd arrived on a wide, gently undulating plain. A few miles away there was a dense deep-green forest, but all around there were scattered stands of trees. The sky was clear and eggshell blue. Rose remembered an ill-fated camping trip with Jimmy Stone to Dartmoor. If you just looked quickly at this scene it might have seemed the same. But there was an uncultivated wildness about this place. The forest was tangled and black as night; the grass around them was tall and crazily wild. Somehow, where Dartmoor had seemed almost cosy in its ruggedness, never that far from cars, roads and hedges, this place felt dangerous and alive.

Rose realised she was grinning like a loon at the sheer joy of it. 'Could this be any more beautiful?'

The Doctor shut the TARDIS door and breathed in deeply. 'That's proper fresh Earth air, that.'

'And this is Bromley?' Rose could hardly believe it.

'They probably don't call it that yet,' said the Doctor. 'Better warn ya – there'll be a lot of wildlife. Wild wildlife.'

They started walking. 'Like what, wolves?'

'Yeah, plus bears, and wild dogs, and mammoths.' He stepped in something and shook his boot. 'And rabbits.' He looked about. 'Das said there was a particular strange tree…'

'Only about 40,000 to check,' pointed out Rose.

She shivered as they entered a wooded thicket. She was wrapped in a thick coat from the TARDIS wardrobe, but the wind still bit at her through it. The Doctor, loping confidently along, seemed unaffected in his jacket and jumper.

'Aren't you cold?'

'Nah,' he said. 'And there'll be humans. The Neanderthals like the forests –' he pointed to it – 'so they'll be over there. Beckenham, Penge way. But your lot, you roam about everywhere. You like big empty spaces cos you're from Africa, the savannah. You jumped down when the trees there died out. Then a whopping great volcano went off, covered the planet in ash. Just a thousand of you left then, you could have just given up, but you set off and conquered the place.'

Rose took his arm. 'Oh, right. So we're not completely useless and evil, then?'

'Not completely. Though you've got a thing about tree-felling.'

Rose smiled. 'Can I just say, I really, really like this place.'

'Of course you do,' said the Doctor as they started down a slope. 'You're adapted for it. This is where you belong, not sat on your behind scoffing Pringles and watching *Loose Women*.'

Rose shivered. 'With the heater on.'

'Yeah. Why d'you think you invented clothes in the first place?'

'And those clothes would be like…'

'Skins. By-product of a heavy red-meat diet.'

Rose laughed. 'What, so everyone in the Stone Age was on the Atkins?'

'No choice,' said the Doctor. 'Mammoth for breakfast, mammoth for dinner and mammoth for tea.'

Something caught Rose's eye. 'Right.' She pointed to it. 'So why's that bloke over there wearing jeans and eating a baguette?'

The Doctor followed her finger. About a couple of hundred yards away there was a long-haired young man in denim flares sitting on a fallen tree, a tin lunchbox on his knee. Even at this distance Rose couldn't help noticing that he was good-looking – not just ordinary good-looking, but Hollywood standard, with Brad Pitt cheekbones and dimples.

'Time traveller,' said the Doctor, 'gotcha.' He strode towards the man, brushing aside branches. 'Oi! I want a word with you!'

The man looked up and Rose was surprised to see the expression on his face. He didn't look alarmed, just surprised and oddly vacant. A second later he dropped his baguette and ran off at an incredible Olympian rate. The Doctor and Rose set off after him, but a few moments later his blue-denimed form was swallowed up by the woodland.

'See,' said the Doctor. 'Open spaces, fast runners.'

'That was too fast,' said Rose, leaning against a tree to get her breath back.

'We know where he was heading, though,' said the Doctor. 'Come on!'

They ran in the general direction the time traveller had taken.

The Doctor was able to track the man by tiny signs: broken branches, trampled grass. Rose's sides ached as she ran alongside him, but she was too exhilarated to care.

About five minutes into their run, they emerged into a clearing surrounded by tall trees. The sunlight dazzled down on them, making Rose squint. The next thing she knew, both she and the Doctor had tumbled into something messy, bringing them to an abrupt halt.

Rose looked down at herself. Her coat was stained with patches of blood and strands of meat. She realised that they had slipped into the carcass of some huge wild beast. Its flanks had been torn savagely apart and its innards almost totally stripped away.

She looked over at the Doctor. 'This is somebody else's lunch, then?'

'Yeah,' said the Doctor, standing up and brushing himself down.

Rose had got the worst of the mess. She stood up and looked down at the huge dead hulk.

'Must have wandered off from the herd,' the Doctor went on.

'Who killed it, then?' asked Rose. 'Neanderthals? Humans?'

'No spearheads.' The Doctor looked closely at the carcass. 'There are teeth marks...' He pointed out rows of serrated marks at the edges of the massive wound in the creature's side.

'So it was another animal,' said Rose. 'And it's still warm, so shall we get going?'

'Hold on,' said the Doctor, turning to her. 'Say "Aaah".'

'Why?'

'Say "Aaah".'

Rose said, 'Aaah.'

The Doctor looked into her mouth and examined her teeth, then compared them to the marks left on the animal. He looked troubled.

Rose closed her mouth. 'What's wrong?'

The Doctor nodded down at the beast. 'Whatever brought her down couldn't have been human. Or Neanderthal. She must have been attacked by a predator.'

Rose guessed what was bothering him. 'But the teeth marks are human? And how's a human gonna kill a mammoth single-handed?'

'How's a human gonna eat a whole mammoth single-handed?' asked the Doctor. 'I know you like your unlimited trips to the salad bar, but…'

Before the Doctor could carry on, there was a rustle in the bushes. Something groaned in the green darkness of the forest, its low cry echoing round the clearing. The Doctor stood very still and gripped Rose's arm tight.

He whispered, 'Whatever it was… it's still here.'

FIVE

'Get ready to run,' the Doctor told Rose. His face was blank, not a muscle moving. He raised a finger very slowly and pointed right. 'You're going that way.'

'And which way are you going?' asked Rose, her heart pounding as another odd, low cry came from the rustling bushes up ahead.

'Don't worry,' said the Doctor, not very reassuringly. 'I wrestled a tiger once.'

'Who won?'

'You just have to rub its tummy,' said the Doctor, even less reassuringly. 'Then it thinks you're its mum and curls up into a playful little ball.'

There was a growl from the bushes.

Rose swallowed. 'That isn't a tiger!'

'I know,' said the Doctor. 'Now, on the count of three. One, two…'

It growled again.

'Two and a half…'

'I'm not leaving you, Doctor,' said Rose.

The Doctor turned to look at her, smiled and said simply, 'You are. Go. Now.'

Rose took a deep breath, tried to smile back and tensed herself to run…

And then suddenly, as so often with the Doctor at her side, the last thing she could have imagined happened.

Loud music started thumping. No, thought Rose, it wasn't just loud – it was deafening, a screech of what sounded like clashing metallic guitars left too near their amps. Instinctively, she flung her hands up to her ears. The bushes where the predator was hiding rustled and she saw, very briefly, a strange grey shape, about the size of a person, flee at lightning speed. But then her attention was drawn to the other side of the clearing, where two men – one black, one white – had appeared.

Again, Rose couldn't help noticing how good-looking they were. She wondered about the special part of the mind that decides who you fancy, and how it kept on working away no matter what danger you were in. They wore flared denim trousers and buttoned jackets, and both had what looked like portable speaker attachments slung over their shoulders on straps, from which the music was blaring. The weirdest thing about them, Rose decided, was their utterly casual manner. They looked as if they were just walking down a high street, and they seemed completely unfazed by the presence of two strangers and the close proximity of some savage beast.

The white man clicked off his speaker and shouted, 'It scares the animals away. They don't like the noise.'

'I'm not exactly grooving along!' cried Rose.

The black man switched off his speaker and silence returned to the clearing. 'I'm sorry!' he called.

Rose took a closer look at the newcomers. They both wore big, colourful metal name badges with large childish lettering, like something off a kids' TV show; the black man was called Jacob, the white man Tom.

'Well, ta,' said the Doctor.

It amused Rose to see him so taken aback by this strange intrusion.

Jacob and Tom looked blankly at him.

'Thanks,' said the Doctor.

What was disturbing Rose in particular was the men's casual acceptance of them. They didn't seem surprised or angry or pleased to find them here. It was as if they weren't giving out any reaction at all.

Jacob strolled slowly up to them. 'You need to take care out here. Haven't you got a stinger?' He brandished the speaker at them.

'Never been issued with one,' said the Doctor. He winked and muttered, 'Do the "own the place" thing,' to Rose, then turned back to Jacob and shook his hand. 'I'm the Doctor. This is Rose Tyler.'

'Hello,' said Tom, smiling. 'I'm Tom and this is Jacob.'

There was an uncomfortable silence.

'Well, that's nice,' said Rose to fill it.

'Have you come to take us home?' asked Jacob. He started to walk on, back in the direction he'd appeared from, and the others fell into step.

'Cos we were getting slightly...' said Tom. He stopped and frowned. 'Oh, what's that word?'

'Worried?' suggested Rose.

'That's it,' said Tom. 'Worried. About the delay.'

The Doctor spoke up. 'Er, gents, that animal. What was it?'

'An animal,' said Jacob.

'One of the dangerous animals,' said Tom. 'We scare them off with stingers.'

'Yeah, but what kind of dangerous animal was it?'

Tom shrugged. 'A dangerous one.' He smiled at Rose, and she couldn't help smiling back. His teeth were perfect. Not just perfect. Immaculate. She'd never seen such a beautiful set.

'You looked a bit strange back there. Afraid,' Tom said.

'Just a bit, yeah,' said Rose.

At the back of her mind she could feel something was wrong and it took her a moment to work out what it was. Then she realised. Normally when you look someone in the eye, you get something back. A tiny non-verbal signal, a kind of spiritual contact. She got nothing from Tom. His eyes remained exactly the same, as if there was nothing inside to interact with. She kept thinking of the immaculately dressed young men who sometimes knocked at the door of the flat with badly photocopied leaflets promising eternal damnation if they didn't turn away from sin, and her mum trying to flirt them into turning to it.

'If you feel afraid again, all you need is combo 410/15,' said Jacob.

Rose nodded. 'Thanks. That clears it all up.'

'We're heading for base, then?' asked the Doctor.

'Yeah, this way. Mind how you go,' said Tom,

pushing through foliage on what was clearly a familiar route.

Rose held the Doctor back a second. 'Are they robots? Or aliens? Or is it too much tartrazine? Or what?'

The Doctor thought for a second. Then he said, 'What.'

A few minutes later they stopped in what appeared to be another area of wild woodland.

'Here we are,' said Jacob.

He walked over to a huge oak tree and knocked a tattoo, a kind of code, on its side. A section of the tree swung up on a squeaky hinge.

Rose was puzzled. 'That's like a Scooby Doo secret door. If this lot are futuristic time travellers, where's the fancy tech?'

The Doctor shrugged. 'Dunno. But that's Das's strange tree. Strange and squeaky.'

They followed Jacob and Tom inside the tree into a small, dark metal compartment that smelled of oil. Rose was reminded of the hospital service lift, a couple of hours back – 28,000 thousand years in the future. She looked over at the Doctor, who was unusually quiet. He seemed troubled and was looking carefully at everything, weighing it up.

Tom thumbed a button on the side of the compartment, which juddered and started to descend with a groan of hydraulics.

There was another uncomfortable silence.

'Your mouth's very big,' Jacob said suddenly.

Rose realised he was talking to her. 'I don't know what to say to that.'

'Where did you get it?' asked Jacob.

Rose looked to the Doctor for help. 'Same place I got my ears,' he said.

'Hmm, they're pretty huge as well. Were they a mistake?' asked Jacob.

'You should sue, getting those,' said Tom. 'My sister Val threatened to sue Face Plus when she got one blue eye, one brown eye. They told her it didn't matter, it was going to be quite fashionable, and she should just take combo 553/22 and get used to them, but she stood her ground and in the end they gave her a refund and three new eyes.'

'You can always do with a spare,' said Jacob, nodding.

Rose decided this was one of those conversations she wasn't going to follow.

The Doctor, slightly affronted, was about to reply when the compartment juddered to a stop. One wall clattered open automatically.

Whatever Rose had been expecting, it wasn't what she found as she walked out. It took her a few seconds to comprehend what she was seeing, just to take it all in. She was looking down from a metal platform into a gigantic cave that must have been several miles wide. Enormous beams of light shone down from what looked like huge circular floodlights; there were six positioned at equidistant points above the cave, suspended on massive hydraulic cables. And what they shone down on was a wooden city.

A variety of panelled wooden buildings were laid out in long, curving streets. Each was slightly different. There were three-storey blocks next to tiny huts, as if whoever had designed the place had had no feel for symmetry or rational planning and had just bunged everything together. It was a cross between a shanty town and a folksy Scandinavian village. A long set of wooden steps led down to the main street, where more people dressed in flared denims were going unhurriedly about their business. Rose heard the gossipy chatter of voices and, distantly, more shouty, bassless guitar music.

Over the main street was a banner on which had been painted in flowery writing 'OSTERBERG: RESEARCH DELIVERING VALUE'.

'We'll take you to Chantal,' said Jacob, starting down the steps with Tom.

The Doctor and Rose followed. 'What is this, Sylvanian Families?' said Rose. 'What's with all the wood?'

'Dunno,' said the Doctor. 'Let's just hope no one invents fire.'

'Normally about now,' said Rose as they climbed down into Osterberg, 'you're filling me in on everything. You know, throwing your arms around and saying, "Well, this is the seventh dominion of Kraal. Fantastic!" or whatever.'

'Yeah, that's what I normally do,' said the Doctor. 'But this time, you see, I've got no idea.'

'Makes a nice change, you not knowing everything,' said Rose.

'Rose, human history stretches over five billion years,' he replied. 'I just don't know this bit. I've got a blind spot for May 1982, but that can't be it. I tell you one thing, forget what Jack said, they're not from the forty-sixth century.'

'How d'you know that?'

'No prongs or pods about, for a start, plus everybody's got hair. And both legs.'

'OK,' said Rose, deciding to let that one pass. 'So, what's our plan? Pretend to be like them?' She gestured to Tom and Jacob and pulled a blanked-out robot face.

The Doctor nodded. 'We find out what's going on before we do anything too drastic. Nice people, I don't like 'em. They can turn nasty.'

'They're weirding me out,' said Rose. 'It's like they're not even curious about us.'

'Exactly. And yeah, I've got no idea why.' The Doctor slapped his arm round Rose. 'Tell you what, we can work it out together for a change.'

They were led along the main street by Tom and Jacob. None of the people of the town gave them a second glance. And there was something else: it wasn't just Tom and Jacob; everybody in the town was startlingly, movie-premiere attractive.

Soon they came to a narrow alley formed by two dangerously sloping roofs. Just as Jacob was about to lead the way down, he was elbowed roughly aside by a man who was quite unlike any of the other residents of Osterberg. To begin with, he was short – only about Rose's height. He was also rather chubby, and about fifty, with a querulous lined face partly obscured by a broad-brimmed hat. He sported a bizarre combination of clothes. A cape was thrown artistically over his shoulder. He wore a smart purple waistcoat, shirt and tie, and a clashing pair of faded combat trousers held up by a piece of string. His feet were encased in scuffed green baseball boots. He stomped off down the alley muttering under his breath, looking to neither left nor right.

Tom and Jacob reacted to him by looking at each other and laughing gently. Rose found that rather sinister.

A few moments later they had squeezed down the alley and through a huge wooden door into a large barn that looked as if it had been converted into an office. The floor was bare, the rock floor of the cave. There were about twenty desks ranged around in an open-plan design, and the people behind them were typing on unwieldy metal machines that weren't quite typewriters but were certainly not computers.

The Doctor and Rose's attention was caught by the man in the hat, who was standing in front of a desk. Behind it, looking almost indecently relaxed, sat an incredibly tall, incredibly beautiful dark-haired woman. Like nearly all the others in the town, she possessed even, symmetrical features, but what really set her off were her eyes. They were a vivid ocean blue, framed by long, exquisitely curled lashes. She wore the uniform denim trousers and a handsomely tailored business suit with large lapels. Her name badge identified her as CHANTAL. Up close, Rose could see that all the name badges had, beneath the name, a small numeric keypad like the one on a mobile phone.

Behind her was a long metal tube connected to a network of similar tubes spread all over the office. There was one above each desk and they eventually snaked out through the wall. The woman Chantal folded a piece of paper, stuck it in an envelope, sealed it and held it under the end of the tube. A whoosh of compressed air snatched it from her hand. Rose remembered her nan talking about a system like that used for sending messages and money in her old job at the Co-op.

Chantal looked up and saw the man in the hat. She smiled. 'Oh. Hello, Quilley. Pleased to see you.'

She had a singsong, faintly accented voice. *Call centre*, thought Rose.

'No, you aren't,' said the man in the hat gruffly.

Chantal quickly pressed some of the buttons on her badge. 'Well, I am now. What can I do for you?'

'It's day forty-nine, Chantal,' said Quilley.

'Yes, and quite a nice day so far. Will you be joining us for drinks later?' She raised her voice. 'We'll be breaking out the peach schnapps this afternoon!'

Everybody in the office except the Doctor, Rose and Quilley cheered and whistled.

Quilley leaned on the desk, virtually spitting in Chantal's face. 'The experiment was only meant to last forty days! Yes, it is day forty-nine, so may I suggest you forget the peach schnapps and try to find out why the heck we are still here?'

Chantal didn't react at all to his anger. 'The Osterberg

Experiment's just been extended, as I told everyone.'

'But why has it been extended?' Quilley's knuckles were white on the edge of the desk.

'Don't worry about it,' said Chantal casually. 'It'll sort itself out in a bit. Now, haven't you got some work to be getting on with? I know I have.'

'I can't stop worrying!' roared Quilley.

'Oh, yes, you can,' said Chantal, still singsong and smiles. 'All you need is a combo in the 662 range.'

'I can live without that!' scoffed Quilley, starting to pace about. He turned and addressed the whole of the staff. 'I can live without your smugness! I can live without your drivel, and I want to know why we're still here!'

He sprang forward, grabbed the desk of the nearest worker and tipped it over. The office workers giggled. The man the desk belonged to just got up from his seat, set it upright again, picked up his typewriter and pencil holder, and sat back down.

Quilley roared and tipped it over again.

The man the desk belonged to just got up from his seat, set it upright again, picked up his typewriter and pencil holder, and sat back down again.

Quilley squared his shoulders and prepared to tip the desk over a third time.

The Doctor grabbed him by the shoulder and said, 'Er, can I make a suggestion? Chill.'

Quilley stared at the Doctor for a full five seconds. Then his attention turned to Rose. Normally she would have found the stare off-putting, but in this place the naturalness of the reaction was a relief.

Quilley turned to Chantal, pointing to the Doctor and Rose. 'Who are they?'

Chantal shrugged. 'Search me, duck. I guess they must have been sent back by the Committee. Late arrivals.'

'Dressed like that?' Quilley looked Rose up and down. 'Her clothes… where did she get them?'

'Why not ask her? She's got a name,' said Rose.

'We both have,' said the Doctor, 'sort of. That's Rose Tyler and I'm the Doctor. You're right, we're late arrivals.'

'Very late,' said Quilley suspiciously.

'Don't let him give you wrong-feeling – it's only what he wants,' said Chantal, as if talking about a naughty five-year-old. She stood up to her full six feet. 'Hello, I'm Chantal. Welcome to Osterberg! Our mission plan is to deliver value by researching human history in a vibrant world-class environment.'

'That's nice,' said Rose, trying to fit in.

Chantal smiled. 'Yes, it is.'

Rose was beginning to find Quilley's lingering gaze irritating. 'Would you mind not staring at me?' she asked politely.

'This is T. P. Quilley,' said Chantal. 'Senior zoo-tech. Better tell you straight, in case you hadn't noticed, and I'm pretty sure you will have, he's a Refuser.'

'Is he now?' said the Doctor, as if that made everything clear. 'Well, Rose here, she's my…'

'Boss,' said Rose quickly.

'My boss,' said the Doctor. 'And she was just saying on the way down your lovely steps how she needed to speak to your senior zoo-tech and go over your research.' He spoke with heavy emphasis. 'She really wants to know what kind of animal we met out there.'

Rose picked up the hint. 'Yeah, I was saying that. Mr Quilley, could you show me your work?'

'Certainly,' said Quilley, who was still looking at her oddly. 'Come on, then.'

He stomped away and a second or two later Rose set off after him.

Quilley led Rose through the winding streets of Osterberg and round a couple of corners to a shack with a porch nailed very ineptly to its front. He pushed open the front door and shooed her in. His staring was, if anything, getting worse. He hadn't said a word to her on their little journey, but every so often he looked over at her, tutted and shook his head. It was starting to annoy her, but she knew the Doctor was relying on her to keep calm and do some digging. It wouldn't be any good to have a go at this old lech.

The big, shady main room of the shack contained a battered settee, a creaking shelf lined with books and a large table on which were scattered more books and a collection of jars. Rose picked one up and saw it contained the pickled heart of an animal. In the corner there was a washing machine, some CDs on a spindle and, strangely, a computer in a glass display case. The computer wasn't futuristic. It looked just like a bog-standard PC of Rose's time. A tattered rug and a small television set, with the detritus of a half-finished meal of bread, cheese and a chicken leg, completed a picture of disorganisation and clutter. The television set was on, showing black-and-white footage of a synchronised swimming team.

In Rose's experience of travels with the Doctor, you could usually sum a place up, however weird, pretty quickly. Things matched, giving you an idea of a new destination's character, and what you might or might not expect to find there. Nothing about Quilley or his room matched the town or the other people of Osterberg. And stranger still, nothing about his own clothes or his possessions made sense in themselves either.

Quilley shut the door and coughed importantly. 'Now, young lady,' he began suspiciously.

'I'd better warn you, try and cop a feel and I'll have your eyes out,' said Rose in a friendly enough tone. She was used to dealing with older men.

'I haven't copped a feel of anything for a very long time, more's the pity,' said Quilley. He continued to observe her as if she was some kind of specimen or curiosity. He sat down and stretched his legs. 'Now. We were supposed to be taken back home nine days ago. And I don't relish the prospect of remaining here in this howling wilderness for very much longer.'

'I don't know anything about that,' said Rose. 'Me and the Doctor, we're just here to join in with your research. Sent by the Committee.'

Quilley raised an eyebrow. 'So you're a zoo-tech like me?' He gestured to a poster on the wall by his bench. On the poster were drawings of a variety of animals – bears, wolves, mammoths.

'Yeah,' said Rose. 'I'm a zoo-tech.' She took off her coat, which was still covered in blood and gore from the dead mammoth. 'Do you mind if I put this in your wash?'

'Go ahead,' said Quilley after a pause.

Rose put the coat in the washing machine. 'So, what kind of animals d'you get here, then?'

'You say you were sent here,' said Quilley, cutting her off. 'Didn't the Committee tell you why the project's been extended?'

Rose was wary of saying anything that might blow her cover. She needed an excuse to get away for a moment and think – she was a terrible liar – and she decided to fall back on one that had served her very well at home when trying to get away from blokes she didn't fancy. 'Look, hope you don't mind, but… I'm bursting.'

'What?' asked Quilley.

'I need the loo.' She pointed. 'Is it through there?'

Quilley frowned. 'You need the what?'

'The loo. The toilet.'

Quilley got to his feet and advanced on her menacingly. 'You weren't sent by the Committee,' he said slowly, shaking his head. 'Who are you?'

'I only wanna use your loo,' said Rose, backing away against the wall.

Quilley came right up to her and barked in her face, 'My dear girl, in the time I come from, nobody's been to "the loo" for 1,000 years.' He pushed his face even closer to hers. 'So what time do *you* come from?'

Week 1
Das's Journal

Jack has asked me to use our computer and put down my thoughts about our first week in the town of Bromley. He says it will be good practice for me at writing.

Writing is something I didn't understand for a couple of days. What it means is that instead of keeping your thoughts in yourself, or letting them out by saying or singing them, you let them out of your head and put them into small markings. But when I grasped it, I learned to understand these markings, which is called reading, very quickly. The words tumbled into my head. Jack says this is because of the Doctor's machine, the TARDIS, which gets inside a person's head and adapts it to understand many different languages, spoken or written. He says this is not magic or the work of gods, and the Doctor is not a god but only very wise. (I think the Doctor is a god and Jack is mistaken here. Jack thinks he knows everything, but he just knows more about this time than me. It doesn't mean he understands life in general at all.)

Jack is very kind for a Them (I must remember to call Them humans). He has a very smooth face, which the other humans seem to like. There is a woman in the flat next to ours who keeps waving at Jack from her window and giving a mating call, and the man who came to install our television kept grinning at him in the same way, and so they went for a walk together.

One of the first things Jack did was cut my hair. Then he went out of the flat and hunted for skins for me. At first I thought the shirts and trousers would be too thin, but I forgot the future is a much warmer time. I have many different shirts and trousers, and things called shoes to protect my feet, but I won't wear socks because they are just stupid. There is no point to them.

I soon realised the strangest thing about my new home. All the hunting is done for you by a tribe of hunters who bring food to the shops. In my tribe, everybody was a hunter, or made the fire, or looked after the children. We only did those jobs. The humans have many different jobs and don't have to think about hunting and food all the time. This means they feel something called boredom. They don't like boredom, but I think it's very relaxing and so they should shut up and count themselves lucky.

Jack brought food from the shops to the flat on our first night in Bromley. He made an invisible fire in the kitchen and we ate cooked meat. Then he gave me afters. I shall never forget it. He passed me a crumbling made-thing called a Bakewell tart. I admit I didn't like the look of it, but he encouraged me to taste it.

I bit into it and then I fainted. The humans make the Bakewell tart by mixing many different kinds of food together. It tastes of the fat of beasts, the goodness of grain and the sweetness of rare, wild fruit, but it is far better than any of those. I don't think I shall ever get used to it. It made me feel happier than I have ever been. I was wrong to fear the future.

When I woke up, I ate all the Bakewell tarts and other things called mini-rolls, and flung my arms round Jack to thank him for bringing them. Jack told me there was no need to eat them all, as there were many, many millions of Bakewell tarts and mini-rolls in the shops. I thought he must be mistaken, as such bounty could only belong to the gods in their shadow-world, but he went out and got more to prove it to me. I ate them, but Jack warned me that as there were so many fatty made-things in Bromley, I would become ill if I carried on.

The plenty in this time is unbelievable. Boredom means you start thinking about other things, not just hunting, because food is always there for you. My thoughts started to race faster and faster, and I had a lot of questions. Jack did his best to answer them but it was hard and tiring for him.

He has decided that before I go out into Bromley I must watch television, which will answer many of my questions. Television is a machine that shows pictures of what all the different human tribes are doing. Each tribe has its own channel and there are many hundreds of channels. I learned numbers by flicking a button to check on the different tribes.

There are tribes that sing and chant, tribes that play games with many different kinds of ball and tribes that fight – as humans still do, the idiots – with things called guns. My favourite television tribe are the Grace Brothers of UK TV Gold. Their purpose is to sell skins to other tribes, but they are not very good at it and there is a crowd in their shop (that we never see) who laugh at them all the time, very cruelly. I hope the Grace Brothers will soon get better at their jobs, or they will run out of money and die.

Jack says I do not understand humour. I don't know what he means.

Captain Jack Harkness's Data-Record

Some anthropologist is gonna love this stuff, probably pay good money for it, so I'm making a record of my progress with the boy that time forgot.

No matter what Rose reckons, bringing this guy up to speed is difficult – but still kind of fun. One of the jokes back at the Time Agency was that people are people; you can go back to any point in human history, anywhere in the universe, and they'll be doing the same old things, making the same mistakes. I know this to be true. There was that girl at a party in Elizabethan London and that proto-humanoid Gloobi hybrid in the wastes of thirty-ninth-century Tarsius who were both happy to make the same mistake with me.

But of course Das isn't quite a human. Thanks to the TARDIS, he took to reading, writing and 'rithmetic like a duck to ducks, but beyond that his brain is wired up in a totally different way. That can be kind of cute at times, but if he's gotta live out the rest of his life here, there are some behaviours he's gotta at least learn to copy, even if he doesn't actually understand them.

OK, so let's make a little list of them. Jokes, especially feel-bad jokes, irony, sarcasm and – bad luck for me – innuendo. Fiction is a biggie problem. To Das, everything's happening now and everything is true. And people never lie, they're just mistaken. Take a look at that last one and wonder again why his lot died out. So it turns out telling lies is the greatest weapon in the human arsenal.

It doesn't help that he had to turn up in this dumbass century. The times between the full mapping of the Earth and the first great breakout into space aren't exactly stirring for the spirit. Everyone either just sits at home or they go camel-trekking in Tunisia or something and call it a big deal. "Woo, let's have a trip round the Greek islands this summer, what an adventure!" – not. No wonder Rose loves exploring so much. The curiosity factor here is zero. They think Mars is exotic, mysterious and far away. Ha. Just two centuries to go until you can get a mortgage right on top of that Face for a bag of Maris Pipers.

I've got him a TV. As those notorious experiments in the forty-second century by Mad King Gary of Kiev proved, you can lock kids in a room with only TV and food aged two and they'll come out sort of fully socialised, if insane, aged fourteen. I reckoned Das could pick up a lot from the boob tube.

But that's where the fiction problem reared its head. I tried to explain the difference between the news (which is supposed to be factual, but in early twenty-first-century Britain that's actually a moot point) and the fictional soaps. But all I got was blank looks. To

Das, Rita Sullivan of Weatherfield and Jacques Chirac are equally bona fide. He still hasn't got the idea that life here is semi-civilised and that if you lose your job you're not gonna get cast out to starve in the wilderness. MTV showed some bimbo in a boy band getting thrown out by his manager and Das pleaded with me to find and save him. And science fiction or anything historical is a real no-no. I had to turn off *Farscape* and *Deadwood* before he saw them and picked up some very mad ideas.

So it'll be a long job, but I'm gonna do it. I'll wow the Doctor and Rose. Three weeks to go – Das is gonna be a fully functioning twenty-first-century boy.

Six

'Ah, here's Lene,' Chantal told the Doctor, shortly after Rose had gone off with Quilley. 'She can show you round properly, fix you up with a room, cos I've got some reports to compile.' She picked up a huge pile of papers bundled up with green string. 'You know, quite heavy stats. Bor-ing.'

So the Doctor went off with the new arrival, Lene. She was as tall and beautiful as all the other women in the town, but as they walked out into the artificial yellow glow of the huge floodlights, the Doctor noticed rings of tiredness under her eyes.

He was rather enjoying not knowing exactly what was going on, but still there was something unsettling about these people that put him a little on the back foot. The strangest thing about them, he had come to realise, was their indifference. Only Quilley had behaved towards himself and Rose in a normal way. Everybody else seemed to simply accept their arrival and their flimsy story, as if they weren't even slightly curious. The Doctor decided to test this indifference. He'd make it screamingly obvious that he wasn't who he said he was and see how the woman reacted.

'Right, Lene,' he said. 'Let's pretend I know nothing

about Osterberg or what goes on in it.'

It was a dead giveaway, but Lene merely asked, smiling and clearly not very intrigued, 'Why?'

'Well, you know, it's a fantastic way of making sure I get up to speed with everything. So, take me through it right from the start...'

'Didn't the Committee brief you?' asked Lene.

'Yeah, of course, but what if the forgetful so-and-sos left something out?' replied the Doctor.

A very faint look of boredom, or irritation, crossed her face. 'Explain everything?' she said grudgingly.

'If you don't mind,' said the Doctor.

Lene tapped a code into her name-badge number panel. A broad, genuine smile lit up her face a moment later. 'Well, I don't now!' she said, suddenly bubbling with enthusiasm. 'Come on, then, Doctor!'

To his astonishment, she took him by the arm and started trotting, almost skipping like a little girl, along the main street, pointing things out on the way. 'This is Osterberg, our little research community. It was built in our time and sent back here with us in it. There are 100 of us – well, 102 now, with you and your boss, Rose. It's named after Chantal Osterberg. You just met her.'

'So she's in charge?' asked the Doctor.

'Yup, she's the boss lady. She's got an intelligence enhancement of plus 810!'

'Bully for her,' said the Doctor, trying to sound enthusiastic.

'So we do everything she says, yes. She joined the team who developed the time engine. And this is the first proper try-out of it. She came up with the notion of using it to travel back to study the past, and put together a team of zoo-techs and anthrop-techs. Us.'

They stopped at a corner. A wooden water wheel was connected to a barrel. Lene leaned over and drank, inviting the Doctor to do the same. As he drank, she started speaking again.

'She chose this time so we could study the Neanderthal people. Discover exactly why they died out. And there are lots of animals to research, and we can take a look at our own human ancestors. But it's really only a test. There'll be many more studies. This is just a start.'

'Oh yeah?' said the Doctor, trying to keep the note of worry out of his voice. 'And what else have you got lined up? As if I didn't know, I mean.'

'Travel back to times with more people about. There are lots of questions Chantal wants answered. What caused the collapse of the European Union? Who assassinated the Mage of Toronto, and why? There's so much we don't know, so many gaps. We might even try going back to the Digital Age. Think what Chantal might learn from that!'

'You keep coming back to Chantal,' said the Doctor as they set off skipping again. 'Aren't you interested in the project?'

'We all had interest patches implanted before we left,' said Lene, 'so of course I'm interested and enthusiastic. We all are.'

'Good,' said the Doctor.

'For Chantal,' added Lene.

The Doctor was about to remark on this when Lene suddenly stopped skipping and took her arm away. She swayed on her feet, put her hand to her head.

'Are you OK?' asked the Doctor.

She snapped out of it, smiled and took his arm again. 'I'm fine,' she said, as if nothing had happened. 'Look in here.'

She led him through a low door into another barn, where a row of workers sat at typewriters watching a bank of black-and-white television screens.

'We've got hidden cameras wired up to collect information. We have to hide away down here most of the time, as we don't want to disturb the people up top. Chantal says if we all went up and mixed with them we'd ruin the experiment.'

She pointed to one of the screens, which showed a murky monochrome view of Neanderthal people gathered around a fire in the heart of the forest. 'That's the Neanderthal camp. Quite lively, them.' She then pointed to another screen, which showed a cave opening in a sloping hillside. 'That's where the nearest humans live. They must be asleep right now. Sometimes they don't get up till about two in the afternoon. To tell the truth, Doctor, they don't do very much.'

'Quelle surprise,' muttered the Doctor to himself. 'You've been outside, though?'

'Once,' said Lene. 'I went on a trip to collect specimens of flora.'

'And?' the Doctor pressed her, trying to get a reaction. Any reaction.

'It was all right,' said Lene. 'I found out quite a lot.'

'For Chantal?'

'Of course.'

The Doctor frowned. He was beginning to get an idea about these people. Now he needed to confirm it. 'But you weren't passionate, excited? You weren't dying to get out there into another time, be one of the first to leave a footprint in the soil you were never born to tread?'

Lene shrugged. 'Just work, isn't it? And I had to get back. Chantal was having some drinks and I wanted to wear my new blouse.' She teetered about for a second, grabbing the edge of a table to steady herself.

'Lene, what's wrong?' asked the Doctor.

He watched her tap another code into her name badge.

'It's fine, I'm fine. I can work for a bit longer, but I'm not gonna be exactly brilliant.'

'You should put your feet up,' said the Doctor.

'Why would I do that?' asked Lene. 'Sorry, Doctor, I'm going to terminate soon anyway.' She pulled herself together and beckoned him out of the door. 'Come on, there's more to see.'

The Doctor stopped her. 'You what? Terminate? Do you mean you're gonna die?'

Lene giggled. 'That's a funny old word.' She reached out and playfully chucked the Doctor under the chin. 'You know what? You sound like a Refuser, you do.'

Rose had decided to tell the truth. At least Quilley behaved like a human being, even if he was the kind who invaded your personal space.

'The early twenty-first century…' mused Quilley.

'Yeah,' said Rose. 'Is that good or bad? And could you get your breath out of my face?'

Quilley stepped back. 'A time traveller from the early twenty-first century…' He stopped and pointed at her. 'My child… you put your jacket in there.' He gestured to the washing machine. 'Why?'

'It's a washing machine,' said Rose.

'A washing machine,' Quilley repeated. 'So not a votive offering to the goddess Maria Vidal, then?'

Rose shook her head. 'What gave you that idea?'

Quilley waved a hand airily. 'This is a small selection from my collection of historical artefacts. I've studied their designs and possible functions for many years. I dress in the manner of the past. I brought some of these objects here to make myself feel at home. Many of them, I think, come from your time. Which must've been very much more advanced than I thought if you had time travel.'

'We didn't,' corrected Rose. 'It's only me that does that.'

'How marvellous!' boomed Quilley. 'Well, I got that right, then.' He hobbled over to his collection and indicated the discs on their spindle. 'Now, what are those?'

'CDs, DVDs,' explained Rose.

Quilley frowned.

'You play them.'

Quilley shook his head. 'Please explain.'

'They've got music or films on them.'

'On them?' Quilley looked baffled. He took one from the spindle. 'So they aren't counters in a game? I thought you...' He mimed a throwing action.

Rose shook her head. 'Look, I really have to go. I mean – go. To the loo.'

Quilley took a packet of pills from his pocket and pushed one out of the foil into her hand. 'Have one of these. It absorbs and recycles the waste products. One of the few drugs I'll take. Saves a lot of bodily unpleasantness but doesn't cloud the mind.'

Rose really didn't like the sound of that. She looked down at the pill, weighing up her dilemma. Then a familiar northern voice said, 'Go on, Rose. There are no toilets, so it's either that or you find a lamppost.'

She turned to see the Doctor standing in the doorway, leaning against the frame with an expression that was half wry, half troubled.

Rose swallowed the pill. It tasted of nothing and slipped down almost disturbingly easily. A second later her desire to go to the loo vanished. 'I dread to think what just went on down there,' she told the Doctor, then gestured to Quilley. 'By the way, I messed up our cover.'

'That's all right. No one'd care anyway,' the Doctor said, moving into the room. 'And you'll be pleased to hear I've worked it out. When these people are from.'

'If I could, I'd wet myself with excitement,' said Rose, grinning. 'Go on, then, do your stuff.'

The Doctor smiled back and gave a mock self-important cough. 'The Great Retrenchment – about AD 436,000. There was a massive space battle over in

Monoceros, between Kallix Grover and the Sine Wave Shrine of Shillitar. Try saying all that with a mouth full of cornflakes. Anyway, Earth got caught in the crossfire. A massive reef of magnetic energy missed its target, drifted billions of miles off course at about a million times the speed of light and smacked into Earth. Wiped every computer, every last scrap of recorded data. And by that time there was a computer in everything. Toasters, tables, grass, air molecules, even people's heads. A vast grid of nanotechnology that curled up and died in under a second.'

'Did they try turning it all off and turning it all back on again?' asked Rose.

The Doctor nodded. 'The IT people did their best. But that just made things worse. There was fire, plague, famine, war. So much was lost. The planet got cut off from its colonies. It was 10,000 years before they got themselves together. A new Dark Age, and this lot of charlies come from it. The after-effects of the reef mean no computer, not even the most basic digital device, worked for millennia. So they turned to different forms of technology. Analogue.'

Rose realised Quilley had leaped for a pencil and paper and was trying to write this all down. 'You're going too fast for me. You're solving the great mysteries of human history and I've got to write this all down!'

'See?' said the Doctor. 'Write it all down. Paper, books.' He crossed to the spindle of CDs and DVDs and picked one up. 'Everything digital was lost for thousands of years.' He checked the label. 'Even

Coldplay.'

'Every cloud…' said Rose, then a thought occurred to her. 'But they can travel through time, so they can't be that dumb.'

'Using dead-end analogue rip engines. Which is even worse than normal rip engines. And they don't strive to create anything better, anything cleverer. Their whole attitude is "that'll do".' He reached into his pocket and took out one of the name badges. There was no name on it, just the small keyboard. 'Because of these. I nicked a spare on the way over.'

'Will you please slow down!' shouted Quilley. His pencil had snapped as he tried to keep up with the Doctor.

'I never slow down,' said the Doctor. 'Biology and chemistry became their big sciences. They can do anything with the body – they know it inside out. They can do anything to it. They could probably take you apart and put you together again. And the body includes the brain.' He waggled the badge under Rose's nose. 'Pharmacology. They've mapped out the brain with incredible precision. Must have taken them centuries of study without computers. So they know how the chemical transmitters in the human brain, that incredible machine, work – down to the tiniest detail.'

Rose took the badge and looked at it. On the back were two small pads and a small triangle.

'That little triangle contains tiny amounts of a vast pharmacopoeia of chemicals. You hook it up to yourself –' he demonstrated by placing it against his own chest – 'and if you're feeling sad, or scared, or frightened, or anything you don't like, no problem! You can send a specific chemical signal to block it. You're fine. Everything's just fine, fine and dandy, hunky-dory.'

Rose couldn't work out if he was angry or impressed.

'There's a woman out there,' the Doctor went on, 'she's gonna die in three weeks. Rose, she just doesn't care.'

'This is amazing stuff,' said Quilley, getting a replacement pencil. 'Could you go back to "every last scrap of data". How do you spell data? And, er, what does digital mean? We know about the Digital Age, but all the printed material about it was lost.'

Rose ignored him. 'And they've found a way to stop people going to the loo.'

'Swift would've loved that,' said the Doctor. 'The human race, with all its wit and intelligence, finally unchained from the lavatory. Yeah, they can control all the functions of the body. They know every gene, they've bred themselves into beauties. Knocked out the genes that cause ageing, introduced genes that cure almost everything, with regular updates sprayed out to keep everyone healthy. They still die in the end, but with the drugs why should they care? Grief and sorrow boiled away, till they're just old mad words.'

Rose struggled to get her head round these revelations. 'They're not human any longer. It's horrible.'

'It's different,' said the Doctor.

'Too different,' said Rose. 'Look at them, they're like

androids. What's the point of them being alive?'

'So.' The Doctor folded his arms and tilted his head slightly. 'You're in pain, in agony… back home, what do you do?'

'Take a drug,' said Rose. 'But it's not the same.'

'Or you're grieving, and the hurt's gonna last for years, and you'll never be the same again without the person you've lost. And someone offers you a quick way out.' He looked her in the eye. He wasn't angry with her, just interested. Rose had the feeling he was trying to get a handle on the situation himself and was using her as a sounding board. 'You telling me you wouldn't take it?'

'Would you?' asked Rose pointedly, and she couldn't read the Doctor's reaction to that at all.

Quilley broke the silence in his booming actor's voice. 'I refuse to!'

'Guessed that,' said Rose.

'I, T. P. Quilley, am one of the last Refusers,' he continued, rolling the words proudly around his tongue. 'And all my human qualities remain intact. I laugh – ha ha ha! I cry! I feel! I appreciate bitter irony! I get bored and angry!' He gave Rose a playful punch on the shoulder. 'I've even been to the "toilet", as you call it. Twice!'

'And you've got a very loud, irritating voice,' pointed out Rose. 'Not to mention, you keep invading my space.'

'Insults!' cried Quilley. 'I haven't heard an insult since my Elaina died…'

'You refuse to pop the pills?' asked Rose.

Quilley struck a dramatic attitude. Everything he said and did was overdone, thought Rose. Unsurprisingly, if everybody else was a zombie. He had nothing to interact with, nobody to compare his feelings to. A small piece of her heart went out to him.

'Twenty years ago I joined the Refusers,' he said. 'Their numbers were dwindling even then. We used to meet at each other's houses and try, step by step, not to use our popper packs. Many fell by the wayside in the attempt. But Elaina and I were dedicated. We were both students. I was a zoo-tech, while she studied the few remaining books of the time before the Digital Age. I noted the ways of animals. The bouncing joy of the kangaroo. The unforced friendliness of the dog. The padding arrogance of the cat.' He sighed. 'Elaina explained some of the books to me, the old stories that people didn't bother with any longer, told me how the wrong-feelings of people in the old days helped them to savour life.'

'A pair of romantics,' said the Doctor approvingly. 'Fantastic.'

'Exactly!' cried Quilley. 'And we embarked on our romantic journey together. It took many months, as we adjusted and identified the glittering panoply of wrong-feelings. Shame, lust, cruelty, envy!' He glowered at Rose. 'Passion…'

'Whoa, Nellie,' said the Doctor.

'Fear, anger, resentment. And there were so many different shades of resentment – simmering resentment, open resentment, guilty resentment…'

'Please calm down,' said Rose in a small voice.

'I'm sorry,' said Quilley. 'You don't know what this means to me.' His voice cracked and he swept away a tear theatrically. 'Oh, my dear Rose. Come here!' He grabbed Rose roughly and hugged her. 'And you, Doctor!' He pulled the startled Doctor to him, and held both their heads tightly.

The Doctor and Rose caught each other's eyes and laughed at the sheer weirdness of it all.

'You don't know what it's been like all these years!' Quilley thundered. 'Except, of course – you do! At last I have somebody else to feel!'

Rose's eyebrows went up.

'I think he means "feel with",' said the Doctor.

'I hope he means "feel with",' said Rose.

There was a whoosh of air. Chantal, who was picking listlessly at her lunch, brushed the crumbs from her hand and reached for the envelope that had fallen from the tube onto her desk. She slit it open with her paperknife, then took out and read the message inside.

In bold and immaculate copperplate script it said, *CHANTAL – I'm back in now. Still hungry. Can you fix me something? Yours, X01.*

Chantal tidied the envelope away in the breast pocket of her suit and crossed over to her workers' desks. Her eyes flickered inscrutably over the pretty, doll-like faces of her charges. Then she came to a decision.

'Tina,' she called.

A pert young woman looked up. 'Yes, Chantal?'

Chantal beckoned her over. 'Tina, can you be an

absolute love and pop down to the Grey Door for me? Just knock on the door and, when it opens, go inside. Simple.'

Tina smiled. 'Of course, Chantal.' And she set off.

Chantal headed back to her desk and picked up the remaining half of her baguette. She was just crunching into the crust when she became aware that Tina was lingering at the door, looking at her with a puzzled expression.

'Yes, Tina?'

Tina came over. 'Chantal, the last three people who went down to check on the Grey Door for you…'

'Suzy, Maria and Pedro, yes?' said Chantal brightly. 'What about them?'

'I haven't seen them around for a few days,' said Tina falteringly. 'They weren't at last night's party, for example.'

'I think you'll find they were,' said Chantal. 'Don't you remember? Suzy was totally sloshed, and Pedro and Maria were dancing like a pair of idiots. We had a fine time.'

Tina tried to remember. She was sure Pedro, Maria and Suzy hadn't been there, but Chantal was really clever, with an intelligence enhancement of 810. She must be right.

So she said, 'OK,' and set off for the Grey Door.

The Grey Door was set into one wall of the cave and, as its name suggested, was a huge grey metal door. All the outlying huts and barns of Osterberg faced away from it and the overhead lights shone the other way.

There was nobody else around.

Tina walked briskly up to it and knocked. She had no idea what was inside. She didn't care. Her interest patch had been set to typing, so that was the only thing about the project that interested her. She started to wonder why Chantal had chosen her to carry out an errand that she knew nothing about, but the thought didn't go anywhere. It started and then it just kind of drifted away into the back of her mind like a speedy summer cloud.

There was no reply to her knock.

'Hello,' she called brightly. 'It's Tina!'

Something in the mechanism of the Grey Door clicked and it started to open. Tina reflected that back home dangerous things were kept behind locked metal doors, in case people wandered into them and got electric shocks or something. But that couldn't be a significant reflection, so it vanished somewhere in her misty, contented head.

The Grey Door swung open, just a crack.

'Hello?' called Tina. 'Not absolutely sure what I've been sent here for, actually.'

A slimy grey hand with six fingers and a thumb slipped around the open edge of the door and beckoned to her.

The hand gave Tina a wrong-feeling. Her heart started to beat faster and she got a kind of runny sensation down her arms and legs. She'd never felt it before. But she knew it was wrong, so she tapped a general all-purpose relaxing code into her popper pack and felt better straight away.

The hand beckoned again and Tina walked closer to the door.

It snatched her by the shoulder and pulled her inside.

Tina had a really bad wrong-feeling about this. She couldn't see much inside the Grey Door, as it was very dark, and then the owner of the hand bit into her side and she got a very, very wrong pain-feeling.

She had enough strength to reach for her popper pack, which sent a soothing balm into her head, and the pain-feeling evaporated. She guessed she was about to be terminated and wondered why. But it seemed pointless to concern herself with this, so she let the question go.

'I'm fine,' said Tina. 'Everything's fine.'

The last thing she saw in the filthy dark were three skeletons arranged neatly against a wall as if they were sitting cross-legged, with their skeletal hands on their knees. They still had their name badges on: PEDRO, MARIA and SUZY. It looked quite comical.

Then the owner of the hand held her steady, opened its huge mouth and bit her head off.

Week 2
Das's Journal

This was the week I discovered there was much more to this world than Bromley. I asked Jack if I could fly in one of the planes, so he used the Internet and the credit card to buy tickets for us. (I never thought I would be confident enough to fly, but I saw Will and Grace fly in a plane on television, and they were not struck down by the gods for their presumption. This reassured me.)

We hired a taxi to take us to the airport. I thought that planes just flew around Bromley, but the drive took a long time and I realised that Bromley is only a small part of the world. There are many other towns, such as New York, Taunton and Riyadh. I wanted to fly to my favourite town on television, Balamory, but Jack said it was not possible.

During the drive we saw grass and trees, but the humans have cut most of them down and put their car-roads over them. Many humans consider this a bad thing, apparently, but I think it was very wise of them and really livens things up. I sat in the back of the taxi and ate lots of crisps. Jack has given up trying to stop me eating fatty made-things. I eat them not only for the pleasure but because I know the gods will see this time of plenty and curse it, so it's a good idea to eat them while we can. Jack says this is superstition, which is the word he uses whenever he doesn't understand something obvious. He thinks he's much cleverer than he actually is.

The airport is a place of many people. We waited for a long time and then we showed our passports – another one of the identity cards they have here – to a woman who let us on to the plane. (Jack used magic empty paper instead of a passport, which said my name was Das Dimitru and that I was from Romania. I told Jack that he was mistaken about my name, as it is just Das, and that I came from the tribe, but he didn't understand.)

The plane was comfortable and I watched television. Jack told me that the film we watched, about Spiderman, was a story, but the word 'story' doesn't seem to translate.

'Right,' he said, 'right now we are flying on a plane. That's true?'

'Obviously,' I said.

'What if I said, right now we are fighting elephants?'

'You would be mistaken,' I said.

He pointed to the television and said slowly, 'A story is mistaken truth. Spiderman is not real, he's an actor.'

'Actor' is another meaningless word.

'You can't have mistaken truth,' I replied. 'A thing is

either true or mistaken.' But I don't think I got through to him.

Jack showed me forests and snowy lands from the plane window and asked if I was homesick, which was annoying because I was learning to play a computer game called F-Zero and rather enjoying it.

We arrived in New York and drove in a different kind of taxi to our hotel, where we lived for a few days. Jack explained the different kind of money used by Americans, and then we went out and saw things like a giant stone green woman with an ice cream in her hand. We ate food at many different restaurants, although sometimes you have to use a knife and fork. I have to say, cutlery ranks with socks as one of the most pointless things made by humans. What did the gods give you hands for?

Jack was, if anything, even more popular in New York. He made friends with lots of people.

We went to see some people playing music. It was much like it is on television, with everyone packed in and lots of electrical noise. I was a bit nervous at first – it reminded me of the place I first arrived back in Bromley – but I danced in the middle of the crowd and drank lots of fizzy cola. Then we went to a place where you only hear the music, which is made by a man in a corner, electrically, with two black discs and a special hat.

A human girl started dancing with us. She looked very happy and told me her name was Stephanie. I asked her if she'd like to dance with Jack too, but she said he was too good-looking, she preferred her men a little rougher and I had a very interesting face. I suddenly realised she fancied me and didn't know what to do. Now I've been here a while I can tell the difference between different humans, but their low voices and the way they rush and jump about all the time aren't very attractive. And they all have very ugly little noses. So I told Stephanie I was what she would call a Neanderthal, and that I came from the past in a time machine, and for some reason that really put her off and she hurried away.

The next day we got the plane back to London. Our trip to America was fun, but the thought of Stephanie keeps coming into my mind. Jack will leave in another two weeks so I must make friends. And I would like a mate.

Captain Jack Harkness's Data-Record

In his old life, Das lived with the Neanderthal folks back home round a fire in a forest and his world extended about twenty miles at most. I realised he had to get used to the idea that this world's bigger than that.

I guess the Doctor must have felt the same when he took Rose for her first spin in the TARDIS. And when you've travelled, and left a trail of devastated hearts behind you, through as much time and space as I have, one planet in one period becomes a wee bit confining. I had to get away from the British weather anyhow and Das seemed to like American shows the most, so I chose New York.

He's picked up so much and taken it in his stride. When I told him the Earth was a sphere and revolved round the sun, in a solar system at the edge of a galaxy, in a universe of infinite galaxies, he just nodded and said, 'Uh-huh, that makes sense.' He got the Internet in seconds, and learned how to use a knife and fork right away, even though he thinks cutlery is stupid. But when I try to tell him for the thousandth time that

Mrs Slocombe is not a real person, he looks at me as if I was the primitive.

My history's not as good as it should be either. Whenever and wherever I travelled before, I'd make a good study of it before setting off. I knew the London Blitz inside out. But though this is only sixty-odd years ahead, there are some things I goof up. We were halfway to the Brooklyn Poisson-o-Rama on the subway before I remembered it wouldn't be built until the collapse of Inter-Bank. And Inter-Bank hasn't even been built yet.

Also, people here have no idea what's going to last from their culture. You come back and expect them to be grooving along to Van der Graaf Generator and reading Shena Mackay novels. But no, it's all U2 and *The Da Vinci Code*, whatever they are. I spoke to a girl the other day who'd never even heard of Sparks. Wake up, people!

While I'm talking about girls, which is so rare, I can report that Das met one in a club. Or she met him. Some women just get turned on by short, stumpy, hairy guys, I guess. Being Das, when she did the 'Hi, who are you?' routine, he went and told her the truth. Still, if he ever does find a girlfriend, the fact that he's got no waist and talks like Minnie Mouse might scare her off. If only he'd showed up on the planet Celation. They sure aren't so fussy there, as I shudder to recall.

SEVEN

The Doctor disentangled himself from Quilley. 'Your time engine, would you take me there?'

'I suppose you'll want to see if it's as good as yours,' said Quilley. 'You might feel envy if it is. Even simmering resentment.' He looked excited as he led them out.

The Doctor turned to Rose. 'We have to know what's powering their engine, and how Das got into it,' he told her. 'And there's another thing bothering me.'

'What's that, then?' asked Rose, but the Doctor could see Quilley trying to listen in on their conversation as they walked along and indicated that they should remain silent for the moment.

Rose nodded – she got it. The Doctor didn't want to raise in front of Quilley the possibility that after their first journey the people of Osterberg, like Das, would not be able to travel safely through time back to their home. The thought raised so many complications in Rose's mind that she decided, as the Doctor apparently had, not to worry about it yet.

Quilley led them to a middle-sized hut in the centre of the settlement. Inside was a bizarre machine. It looked at first sight like some kind of steam engine.

It consisted of a thick metal tube about six yards long with handles and levers down one side and what looked like a large piston hammering away at one end. It made a dangerous-sounding, insistent rattle. Steam hissed from one end at intervals of a few seconds.

Quilley gestured to it with a flourish. 'Rather impressive, don't you think, Doctor? I bet you're feeling impressed.'

'Impressed at how rubbish it is,' said the Doctor, staring in horror.

Quilley looked puzzled and then laughed loudly. 'You're being sarcastic, aren't you? Marvellous!'

The Doctor bent down to look more closely at the machine.

Rose joined him and whispered, 'He's getting on my nerves.'

'He's not had anyone normal to talk to for years,' said the Doctor. 'He's probably really lonely.'

A cloud of steam blew into their faces and they stepped back.

'A time machine that runs on steam?' queried Rose. 'I can't accept that.'

'You accepted Chitty Chitty Bang Bang. They've got the strangest technology I've ever seen,' said the Doctor. 'Do you want me to explain to you how it works? Only take about five years.'

'I think I'll skip that, then,' said Rose.

'And I need a proper poke at it if I'm going to switch it off without blowing us all to smithereens.' He produced the sonic screwdriver from his jacket.

'And is that gonna take five years?' asked Rose.

'Might seem like it,' said the Doctor. He looked up at her. 'Why don't you investigate our other little mystery: what that creature was?' Then he went 'ooh' at a particular bit of weird technology at the base of the engine and stooped down to examine it more closely.

Rose nodded. 'It might just be a bit more exciting than sticking my head into a colander.'

'All right. Find one of those stingers of theirs and look after yourself.'

Quilley glanced at his watch. 'Reddy will be going out to the Neanderthals in a few minutes. He's our surface observer. Goes up to study the Neanderthals and humans at close quarters. You'll find him by the steps.'

'Won't he mind me going with him?' asked Rose. Then she realised. 'Of course he won't. He'll just go "Yeah, fine, whatever."'

'You're learning,' said Quilley. 'You could stab one of the idiots in the back and they'd just say, "Yeah, fine, whatever."'

'But be careful,' said the Doctor, over the whirr of the sonic screwdriver. 'Won't be the same up there. It's a wild world.'

'You usually tell me not to wander off,' pointed out Rose.

The Doctor smiled at her. 'Go on, wander off. Just don't expect rescuing.'

'So long as you don't,' said Rose, and hurried away before he could change his mind.

*

Reddy was the man the Doctor and Rose had seen eating the baguette on the surface. 'Sorry I ran when I saw you,' he told Rose as they ascended the steps from the town. 'I had a moment of wrong-feeling and didn't know quite what to do. I thought you were probably from the human cave.'

'You steer clear of the humans, then?' asked Rose.

'Yeah. They do odd things, so I move away,' said Reddy. 'They behave strangely for no apparent reason. Part of my interest is to find out why.' He handed Rose one of the speaker attachments from a pack slung over his shoulder. 'The noise makes animals go away, but the humans have got used to it and they don't go away any more.'

A few minutes later they were striding through the woods. Rose couldn't help tensing up at the thought of the ferocious animals that were lurking in its canopied depths, but Reddy, of course, was unconcerned, walking quickly and nonchalantly along a route he seemed to know well.

'What about the Neanderthals?' asked Rose. 'What are they like?'

'Nicer,' said Reddy. 'Obviously they're still a bit strange, quite like Refusers. And their voices are very loud and high. Their language is very easy to grasp if you've had the linguistic interest patch. Have you?'

'Yeah, sort of,' said Rose.

'But they don't seem to have as much wrong-feeling as the humans and they don't talk as much.'

'Right, so they do actually get bothered about things?' commented Rose.

It was the first time she'd really spoken to one of the Osterbergers and, like the Doctor before her, she found their passivity disturbing. She was getting nothing back from Reddy, none of the usual non-verbal signals that give you an unspoken, almost instinctive, reaction to a new person. She realised how terrible it must have been for Quilley living among these people. On her travels with the Doctor she'd met robots with more personality. She thought back to her killingly boring science teacher, how his monotonous drone of a voice and empty stare had almost made her weep in frustration on hot summer-term afternoons, pen doodling aimlessly in the margins of her rough book, and realised what a beautiful, unique human being he had been compared to these jolly, pre-programmed, plasticised people.

'It's quite interesting,' continued Reddy. 'But how anybody can live like they do – the humans or Neanderthals – I do not know. Not being in control of yourself, it must be horrible. And they do this thing called violence. It's a bit disturbing when you first see it. You'll need combo 221/8 to get used to it.'

Rose said, 'And we don't have violence where we come from?'

'Of course not,' said Reddy lightly, expressing nothing more than mild surprise at the obvious oddness of her question. 'Why disagree when you can party?'

Half an hour later they had travelled from the ragged edge of the woods, over the bleak grassy moorland and into the sprawling, densely packed forest the Doctor had identified as the likely home of the Neanderthals when the TARDIS had arrived. The fresh smell of pine almost took Rose's breath away. She felt an illogical and quite embarrassing urge just to hug one of the huge, ancient tree trunks in all its lovely knottiness. The forest was like something out of a shampoo advert: impossibly green, impossibly haphazard, impossibly dark and mysterious, with vents of light peeking through the leaves to make lattice patterns on sudden bright outcrops of daffodils and bluebells. It made her feel strong, alive and young, as if she could do anything here. She suddenly understood why people used to believe in fairies. There was real magic in this place, and as she and Reddy trampled through the bracken she wouldn't have been surprised if a gnome had suddenly popped its head out from under a toadstool.

There was a rustling from up ahead. Reddy took her by the arm and gently pulled her down behind a fallen trunk. 'Look, there's some violence now. Best to keep away when they're doing it. You'll be interested.'

Rose could just make out the figures of two Neanderthal men about 200 yards away. She realised Reddy would have enhanced eyesight and hearing, much better than hers. For all she knew, he might be able to zoom in on the scene.

The Neanderthals were, as far as she could tell, almost identical to Das. They carried long spears and were standing over the body of a freshly slain pig, shouting in their parrot-like voices and pushing at each other. After a few minutes one of them pushed the other to the ground, slung the pig over his shoulder and lurched off deeper into the forest.

'Peculiar, isn't it?' observed Reddy, shaking his head as he got up.

'Just a bit of a squabble,' said Rose. 'You should see Saturday nights where I come from.'

Reddy showed no interest in this remark, simply taking Rose's words at face value and not bothering to ask where she came from. As they moved on he told her, 'I've been coming out here since we arrived, taking photos and making notes.'

'You'll be a big name when you go home,' said Rose politely.

Reddy looked blankly at her.

'You know, famous.'

'More of your strange words,' said Reddy. '"Famous"?'

'Important. Everybody knows you.'

'I see. Like Chantal. I won't, and anyway why would I want that?'

Rose shrugged. 'I dunno. It's a good feeling, for some people. Feeling proud of what you've achieved.'

'Oh, I get it,' said Reddy. 'Like Quilley, wanting to be envied.' He nodded ahead to where the Neanderthals had disappeared. 'Or like those two – they both want to feel proud about the kill when they get back to the camp, so they do the violence thing. You've got a head start on me, as I don't understand proudness. Why did people have it?'

'I dunno, they just did,' said Rose.

'Why, though? What was the point?'

Rose felt she was making a breakthrough. 'You're interested in that? You want to know?'

'Yes,' said Reddy. 'Do you know why there was proudness?'

Rose decided to try something. 'What if I don't tell you?'

Reddy frowned. 'But why wouldn't you tell me?'

'Maybe I'm proud about keeping it secret,' said Rose, trying to goad him. For good measure she poked him in the ribs. 'Come on. React!'

'You're giving me a wrong-feeling,' said Reddy. His hand moved to his popper pack.

Rose knocked it down. 'Don't keep pressing that thing!'

Reddy smiled smugly. 'I see, you're a Refuser. That must make you feel very wrong.'

All Rose's frustrations, encouraged by the natural majesty of the forest, boiled over. She grabbed the popper pack and yanked it off Reddy's chest, then took as big a run-up as she could in the confined space and hurled it overarm into the nearest thick mass of vegetation.

'Why did you do that?' said Reddy simply. 'I'll never find it.'

'Just try it,' said Rose. 'Try a bit of wrong-feeling.'

'But I don't want to,' said Reddy.

'It scares you,' said Rose. 'That's a start. You wanna know why these people behave the way they do? Try it yourself!'

Reddy stood open-mouthed, staring into space for a full thirty seconds. Then he blinked and looked up at

Rose. 'That's really clever. Why didn't I think of that?' For the first time, his wet, simple smile was clouded with wonder.

The odour of woodsmoke and the sound of voices led them to the Neanderthal camp. Rose pushed through a particularly tangled mess of branches and suddenly found herself in a clearing the size of a large suburban garden. There seemed to be about forty Neanderthals. Many were gathered round a large bonfire in the centre of the clearing. A smaller group of males and females sat making spearheads in one corner, chipping away at lumps of flint with small hand-tools. Some other men were skinning and preparing the dead pig, which on closer inspection Rose realised was an enormous wild boar. Some children were playing with little dolls made from twigs, being supervised by a young female with all the patience of a nursery teacher. She looked up as they entered and smiled, displaying a row of gleaming white teeth.

'Reddy!' she cried, waving.

Rose winced. Her voice was even higher and more piercing than Das's. To her surprise, the others in the camp barely paid them a second glance. They were obviously accustomed to Reddy's visits.

Reddy led Rose over to the girl. 'Hello, Ka,' he said, nodding curtly. Rose was astonished to see him lean down and give the Neanderthal girl a quick peck on the cheek. She was also put out when the girl, Ka, shot her a look of suspicious disquiet. It was a look Rose knew well – what are you doing with my boyfriend?

The implications of it made her head reel.

'This is Rose,' said Reddy quickly. 'And she's not my girlfriend, before you get any ideas.'

Ka's face perked up and she shook Rose's hand. 'Oh, you're pretty for a Them,' she said. 'Very clean.'

On the back foot, Rose just smiled back and said, 'Thanks.'

'Are you from Osterberg too, then?' said Ka, slipping her hairy arm casually through Reddy's.

'Yeah,' said Rose, 'kind of.' She found herself instantly warming to Ka.

'Well, I knew you weren't from the Cave obviously. Sorry,' said Ka. Then she called out to the rest of the camp, 'Everybody, this is Rose. Another of the Good Them from Osterberg.'

There was a general cry of greeting and some applause.

'Ta,' said Rose, rather overcome. She didn't know quite what to do, so she just waved.

The Neanderthals laughed kindly.

'Hey, you two should come and see this!' said Ka. She led Rose and Reddy through a tangled path of branches at the opposite side of the camp. 'You said you wanted to take some photos when this happened. Sakka's having her baby!'

They emerged into another, much smaller clearing, where a female was lying on her back, arms flung around her head. An older female, in the role of midwife, was pouring water from a rough stone bowl over her forehead and whispering soothing words. A male – obviously the expectant father – sat cross-legged at the edge of the scene, looking up occasionally and biting his nails.

'Come on, love,' he said, 'give it another push.'

'I'm trying,' said Sakka, groaning.

'Yeah, just butt out for a minute,' said the midwife, gently but firmly. 'We're nearly there.'

Rose wanted to jump with glee at the bizarre ordinariness of it all. The Neanderthals' acceptance of Reddy felt odd, but then she remembered seeing TV footage of tribes in her own time that had just made contact with the outside world and took all its wonders in their stride.

The midwife looked up and glanced at Reddy. 'You're just in time. Get your camera out quick.'

'Are you sure you don't mind?' asked Rose considerately. She felt quite certain that if she were ever in a similar position, having photos taken would be the last thing she'd want.

Reddy stepped back and started to get his camera out of his pack. He looked over at Rose and swallowed. His behaviour was already getting more normal, after only minutes without the popper pack. 'I need combo 754/3,' he whispered.

'I don't, so why do you?' asked Rose.

Reddy lowered his voice. 'This is going to be a bit disgusting.'

'Most natural thing in the world.'

'Exactly,' said Reddy. 'I'm getting too much wrong-feeling… This is a mistake. I should go back. I don't want to understand if it feels like this.'

Rose considered. 'Back home we give birth, don't

we?' she asked rhetorically, hoping she was right. 'Get pregnant? It's just the same.'

'It's not like this,' Reddy hissed. 'Have you ever been pregnant?'

'No,' said Rose.

'Well, I have,' said Reddy emphatically. He gestured to the groaning Sakka. 'And it was two days of bliss. Nothing like that.'

The Doctor finished his examination of the engine at last. He emerged from the underside and stretched his long legs, only to discover Quilley asleep against a wall. He walked over and gently flicked him on the nose.

'Something's bleeding power off the engine,' he said.

Quilley woke with a start. 'Oh, Doctor,' he said, momentarily disoriented. 'Just resting my eyes. I was having a most marvellous dream, filled with sensation –'

'Please don't go on,' said the Doctor, interrupting him. 'That's probably gonna be really boring.' He then smiled and pointed to a thick metal pipe that ran from one end of the engine into the far wall. 'The engine's fully powered up. Not just ticking over, like it should be. And most of the power it's producing goes down there. So where does that lead?'

Quilley said nothing.

'Eh?' demanded the Doctor.

Quilley shrugged. 'How do you expect me to know? I'm a zoo-tech. Ask me how to fix up an elephant with diarrhoea or something.'

'I know that already,' said the Doctor. 'So where's your engineer?'

Quilley looked puzzled.

'Engine-tech? Mech-tech?' suggested the Doctor.

'Mech-tech,' Quilley confirmed. 'I asked Chantal that. The Committee said we didn't need one. It's all being worked from their end.' He studied the Doctor's expression. 'That look on your face makes me start to wonder if they know what they're doing.'

'Breaking news – they don't,' said the Doctor. 'But someone here's a mech-tech, all right.' He pointed to where the pipe curled into the engine and indicated a patch of dull silver scarring. 'This has been soldered recently, since you came here anyway.' A thought struck him. 'I don't suppose you've got a plan of this town?'

Quilley delved into a pocket of his waistcoat. 'Here you go. Came with the welcome pack.'

The Doctor took it eagerly and unfolded it neatly over the top of the engine. He located the engine room and traced a line across from it with a long index finger. 'OK, so the pipe must lead… there.' He tapped at an unmarked section, a small blank area at the edge of the cave. 'What's that?'

'That'll be the Grey Door,' said Quilley. 'Now that you mention it, you're right, there is a big pipe going into the side of it.'

'Oh, the Grey Door,' mused the Doctor. 'And what's behind the Grey Door?'

'I assumed it was just some more of this mechanical

gubbins,' said Quilley.

The Doctor sighed and folded up the map. 'But you never bothered to have a look?'

'Why would I?' said Quilley. 'I've spent most of my time here studying mammoth droppings.'

'Fantastic,' said the Doctor with heavy irony. 'The only person in Osterberg with any potential for natural initiative and you just happen to be one of those people who haven't got any natural initiative.'

'It's only a ruddy pipe,' said Quilley. 'So, is it significant?'

The Doctor was already heading out of the engine room. 'Yeah. Could be very significant.'

'I'm excited,' said Quilley, hurrying a little to keep up. 'Are you excited?'

The Doctor considered. 'I'm worried and excited.'

Quilley's eyes lit up. 'You can do both at the same time?'

'Better than that. Right now I'm worried, excited and curious.'

Quilley thought for a second. Then he slapped the Doctor heartily on the back and roared, 'So am I!'

The tiny Neanderthal baby screamed and kicked at the sky. Rose watched as the midwife leaned over and in a routine way bit decisively through the umbilical cord and then poured water over the child. 'It's a girl,' she told Sakka soothingly.

Sakka sat up just a little, her head cradled by the father, and took the baby into her arms.

What lies ahead for that little girl, Rose wondered,

born into a race that would, in a short while, disappear for ever? She longed to be able to point these trusting people to a bright future, but she knew there was no hope. Their species was going to die. She wasn't sure how close this was to the end for them. Perhaps these individuals could make it through…

She tried to push the thought to the back of her mind and knelt down to share the Neanderthal family's happiness. It didn't feel like an intrusion.

The midwife took her hand. 'Are you a wise woman of Them?'

'Well, don't know about that, but I'm not totally thick,' said Rose.

The midwife gently stroked her cheek. 'Your skin's soft, like Reddy's. He's a good man. You're not like the Them from the Cave.' She hesitated for a second, then asked plaintively, 'Do you know why they hate us?'

'I've no idea,' said Rose truthfully. 'I don't know how anybody could.'

She remembered her task for the Doctor and asked, 'Oh, do you know a man from here called Das?'

'You've seen him?' The midwife's eyes lit up. 'We thought he was dead, killed by Them or an animal. Where is he? Where's he gone?'

Rose swallowed and tried her best to lie. For once it would probably be easier than telling the truth. 'He told me to tell you he's OK and not to worry about him. He won't be coming back, but he's happy where he is. It's a good place.'

To her own ears she sounded faltering and unconvincing, but the midwife clearly believed her.

'I must let everybody know,' she told Sakka. 'Everything's fine now. You just lie there for a while.' She got up and hurried back into the main clearing, crying, 'Rose has brought news about Das! He's fine!'

Feeling guilty, Rose nodded awkwardly to the young couple and backed out into the bushes. She could hear the cries of excitement and relief from the Neanderthals as the midwife's news spread, and pangs of regret and shame burned in her heart. She had never felt more ashamed of being human.

Because it was humans who were going to slaughter these people – and they were people – to extinction.

She looked around for Reddy, who had backed off quickly after taking a few photographs. A flash of denim blue in the trees a little way distant caught her eye and she was just about to call out to him when something stopped her. Reddy was kissing Ka. Not a quick peck this time. A full-on snog with tongues.

Rose crept up, trying to keep herself hidden behind a tree trunk. She risked a peek and saw that Ka had broken the kiss and was smiling up at Reddy.

'I've been wanting you to do that ever since you first came here,' she said. 'And I thought the boys here were slow on the uptake! Could I have flirted any more obviously?'

'Flirted,' said Reddy slowly. 'We don't have that word.' He caressed her cheek, nuzzling his face in her hair. 'You know, we really shouldn't be doing this…'

Ka pulled a mischievous face. 'That's what makes it good. No one from our lot's ever kissed a Them before.'

Reddy bit his lip and flushed. It was the first sign of

humanity Rose had seen in any of the Osterbergers but Quilley. 'This is a wrong-feeling and a good-feeling, all at the same time.' He traced his fingers delicately over Ka's features. 'Where I come from, when we kiss it isn't like that. We take combo 934/77 now and then, and pair up with whoever's nearest.'

Rose raised both eyebrows. Well, at least that answered one question she'd been dying to ask.

'You don't love?' asked Ka, fascinated.

'Yes, that's combo 857/87,' said Reddy. 'But it's nothing like this.'

They kissed again.

Rose gave herself a big thumbs-up. Twenty minutes off the drugs and Reddy was turning normal, kissing an inappropriate girl. As the couple slid gently to the ground and started pawing each other, Rose realised this was the sort of private occasion you really didn't want to intrude on and started slipping away.

And then, without warning, there was a great commotion.

It happened too quickly for Rose to take it all in. Several things seemed to occur at once. There was the noise of the forest being invaded: branches cracking, running feet, and yells – low-pitched, human yells. The Neanderthals leaped up in fright as one, several of the men grabbing their short spears. And then cavemen – real human cavemen – burst into the clearing.

They were bearded, dressed in skins and smocks, their faces dyed blue. Several whirled primitive axes, while others carried long spears, which they let fly through the air. Rose watched as a Neanderthal man was caught by a spear and crashed to the ground.

It was the invasion of the humans. With their casual laughter and bullies' gusto, they reminded Rose of nothing so much as football hooligans. Furious, she reached for her stinger, aimed it into the clearing and twisted it on at full volume. The thrashing metal boomed out over the scene.

She realised this was a bad idea very quickly. Instead of frightening the humans, it attracted them to her. A couple of the invading men burst through the bushes and grabbed her, knocking the stinger out of her hands. She kicked and punched to no avail. One of the laughing men held her still, then the other took what looked like a hide sack from inside the skin he was wearing and pulled it over her head.

Rose tasted her own blood in her mouth. The musty smell of the sack overpowered her and, just as she felt herself being lifted up and carried off, she blacked out.

The Doctor ran his hands over the huge locking mechanism of the Grey Door. It was a rectangular metal box built into the door itself. He whistled. 'Now that's what I call a lock.'

'Ah, we call it that too,' said Quilley.

The Doctor produced the sonic screwdriver from his jacket and held it proudly in front of Quilley's face. 'So what do you call this?'

'A pen,' said Quilley.

'Wrong,' said the Doctor, and set to work. The tip of the sonic screwdriver lit up with its familiar blue glow and it buzzed busily.

'I suppose there's a computer in that, then,' said Quilley.

'There are twenty-nine computers in it,' said the Doctor. He stopped for a second and put his ear to the lock. 'Hang on a second. Did you hear that?'

'That awful buzzing, yes,' said Quilley.

'No, not that,' said the Doctor. 'Coming from inside.'

Quilley pressed his ear to the door.

Very faintly a woman's voice said, 'Hello…'

'Hello,' the Doctor called back. 'Who is that?'

The voice said quietly, 'Chantal sent me down here to the Grey Door… but there's something wrong… I'm feeling wrong now… Please let me out…'

Quilley clicked his fingers. 'That's Tina. She's one of the note-techs from the control centre.'

The Doctor activated the sonic screwdriver again and set to work with renewed urgency. 'I'll be with you in five seconds!' he called in. 'Don't worry.'

The lock was a difficult one, typical of the cumbersome and archaic technology of Osterberg. Its innards contained a series of interlocking bolts and springs that the Doctor had to unpick by feeling their responses to the screwdriver's sonic waves, one by one.

The timid, frightened voice spurred him on. 'Come on!' he urged himself.

'Please help me,' said the voice, lost and childish-sounding. 'There was something in here, something – I don't know the word – it caused pain and wrong-feelings…'

'The poor girl,' said Quilley. 'She's got no understanding of pain.'

'I'm nearly there,' said the Doctor.

'Please open the door. It's dark,' said the voice. The Doctor performed one final adjustment to the sonic screwdriver and there was a satisfying click from the lock mechanism. 'There!' he cried.

He grabbed the edge of the Grey Door and with an effort swung it open. Nothing and nobody came out. Inside was pitch blackness.

'Tina,' called the Doctor softly. 'Tina, you can come out now.'

Something was hurled out through the door almost contemptuously. It took the Doctor a moment to realise, as it clattered to the rocky ground of the cave, that it was a human skeleton. It was still partially clothed in scraps of blue denim. The name on its badge was TINA.

Quilley looked up at the Doctor. 'But she was only talking to us a moment ago…'

The Doctor had turned a little paler than usual. 'I think I'm gonna shut this door,' he said.

He started to swing it slowly to. Then, with a startling abruptness, a slimy grey six-fingered hand emerged from the darkness and started to push it the other way. The Doctor engaged with his unseen opponent, struggling against it to close the huge metal door.

'Come on!' he shouted over his shoulder to Quilley.

'This must be real fear, mustn't it?' said Quilley in a small voice.

'Terror, technically,' said the Doctor. 'Any chance of a bit of courage?'

'I'll try,' said Quilley, and joined the Doctor, taking a firm grip at the edge of the door. He strained his under-exercised muscles, flinging his entire weight against the slowly shifting metal…

Just as the Doctor thought he might actually succeed in closing the Grey Door – as the gap narrowed to a fraction of an inch and the ugly hand appeared to lose its grip – the creature on the other side redoubled its efforts. The door burst fully open and he and Quilley were sent reeling backwards onto the floor. The Doctor realised that the struggle had been a sham. The creature was incredibly strong and had been playing with them, allowing them a moment of hope before it emerged.

He looked up. It was at least seven feet tall and appeared to be vaguely humanoid, with a head, two arms and two legs. It looked strangely lumpy and unfinished, as if its grey, putty-like skin hadn't quite settled yet.

There were two particularly strange things about it. The Doctor had expected a ferocious, snarling beast, but the expression on its ugly, sunken-cheeked face was one of playful politeness under a full head of glossy, neatly parted hair. And it was dressed in a smart black suit, with a long grey tail lashing like a whip from an opening in the seat of its trousers.

'Thank you for opening the door,' it said mockingly in Tina's voice. 'Did you like my impersonation?' Then its voice changed to a rasping croak. 'Are you humans? Are you humans?'

EIGHT

The creature's eyelids flicked rapidly. It was staring straight at the Doctor. No, not staring, he realised – it was squinting, as if its eyes were getting adjusted to the light. He thought of the tiny, gummed-up eyes of baby mice, and that gave him an idea as it asked again, 'Are you humans?'

He pulled himself up to his full commanding height and replied in an equally commanding and disdainful tone, 'Of course we are not humans.'

The creature continued squinting, viscous tears of concentration pouring from its eyeballs. 'Are you sure?'

'Of course I am sure,' said the Doctor. He pointed to the Grey Door. 'You are not ready. Return behind the door.'

'But I'm still hungry,' the creature wheedled. 'Tina was nice, but not very filling.' It pointed to Quilley. 'That looks fat and tasty. Is it a pig?'

The Doctor shot a quick glance at Quilley, who was shaking with fear.

'We are not humans or pigs,' he said importantly. 'We are superior. To humans and to you.' He licked his lips. 'We might eat you, since we're hungry too.'

The creature started back towards the door and the Doctor began to relax. Then it whirled round. 'Humans lie!' it squawked. 'You could be humans, and lying!'

Quilley whimpered. 'Are you insane?' he whispered to the Doctor.

'Barmy, but this is one of my lucid moments,' the Doctor whispered back.

The creature took a step forward. 'Are you lying?'

The Doctor thought quickly. 'Can a human do this?' he asked proudly. The sonic screwdriver was still in his hand. He brought it up and activated it, pointing it at Quilley. Quilley's hat spun off his head and onto the Doctor's. 'Humans cannot move a part of their head to another human, can they?'

The creature pondered, looking suspiciously between them, then at the hat, then finally at the sonic screwdriver. 'What is that appendage?' it demanded.

'My silver hat-swapping finger,' said the Doctor coolly. 'You don't have one, do you? Neither do humans.' He levelled it at the creature threateningly. 'Now, get back inside before I use it on you!'

The creature gave a little cry and then bolted back through the Grey Door.

The Doctor immediately leaped forward, slammed it shut and locked it with the sonic screwdriver. Then he turned, leaned on the door and beamed. 'Not bad,' he said. 'Like any animal, it'll only attack if it reckons you're not a threat. I convinced it we were, so it stopped bothering. Good job it was a baby one.'

Quilley's legs gave way and he sank to the floor. 'But

what was it? It's like no animal I've seen.' He coughed. 'Plus taking specimens isn't allowed.'

The Doctor popped the hat back on Quilley's head. 'That isn't a specimen. And that creature never walked the earth. Someone here made that thing, using your technology. Genetic engineering. And who would have the initiative to do a thing like that, hide it away in its own metal womb with a supply of power to make it grow?' He hauled Quilley up and said significantly, 'Only someone who wasn't popping the pills.'

'I'm the only Refuser here in Osterberg,' said Quilley. 'You don't think I would have wasted the time and effort on bodging something like that together?'

The Doctor gave him a searching look. 'No, I don't,' he said at last. 'So you aren't the only Refuser, are you?'

He started to stride away, heading in the direction of the town. Quilley gathered himself together, settled the hat back on his head and followed.

Three figures were walking towards them, silhouetted against the light. The Doctor identified Jacob and Lene, walking with the usual casual shuffle of the Osterbergers. In the centre, walking with characteristic confidence and purpose, was Chantal.

'You took a silly risk opening that door, Doctor,' she said lightly. 'The Hy-Bractor could have devoured you, which would have been a shame, because I'm very interested in you.'

'Hy-Bractor...' The Doctor mulled over the word. 'You're its mother, then. Why?'

'That isn't your concern,' Chantal replied smoothly.

She held up a small black box. 'As you're so clever, Doctor, know what this is?'

'Duh… remote control?' said the Doctor.

'Yes,' said Chantal. She indicated a knob on its surface. 'I twist this and a radio signal gets sent to the popper packs worn by Jacob and Lene here. I'm going to do it now.' She twisted the knob. 'Quilley, you know that violence thing they do up top, the primitives?'

'Of course I do,' said Quilley uneasily.

'I'm very sorry,' said Chantal, smiling, 'but I've brewed up the combo that causes it. And it works very nicely with the patch that makes them do everything I say.'

Jacob and Lene advanced, their faces suddenly contorted with anger. They had long wooden truncheons in their hands.

'But if you just relax, there shouldn't be very much wrong-feeling,' said Chantal. 'Alternatively, come with me. Then there'll be no wrong-feeling again, for either of you, ever. The offer's there…'

The Doctor pretended to consider, grabbed Quilley's arm and shouted, 'Run!'

They set off at a furious pace, the Doctor virtually hauling the terrified and confused Quilley along the dark side of the cave, away from the Grey Door. He had a plan to circle the edge of the cave and reach the steps on the other side. He risked a glance backwards – and saw that Jacob and Lene were, impossibly, almost upon them, faces contorted with rage and hate, snorting and growling like animals. The genetic perfection of the Osterbergers made them incredibly healthy and they ran with the ease and grace of wild things.

Quilley was clubbed first, going down under a savage assault from Jacob. The Doctor attempted to pull Jacob off, but then felt the inevitable smack of the truncheon wielded by Lene against the back of his skull. He fell protectively over Quilley.

Jacob and Lene snarled and gloated over the unconscious bodies of the Doctor and Quilley, as one raising their truncheons to deliver death blows. Chantal sauntered up, twisting the knob on her remote control, and their arms instantly fell to their sides. Beatifically empty smiles returned to their faces and they looked down, confused at what they had done.

'Chantal, why did we do that?' asked Jacob.

Chantal pointed the remote control and sent a dose of general warm, well-being into their bodies. 'Because doing what I tell you makes you feel nice,' she said perfunctorily.

'That's true,' said Lene, laughing.

Rose was dimly aware that somebody had pulled the bag off her head and that somebody else was giving her a sip of water. The sweaty stench of the bag lingered in her nostrils and she fought back an urge to throw up.

Then her consciousness suddenly kicked back in and the meaningless colours, sounds and shapes around her resolved into clarity.

An old woman was stroking her face. She looked at least eighty and her sharp, pointed features were framed by a riot of curly grey hair. She wore a collection of skins much like those worn by the Neanderthals.

'Ooh, ain't she pretty, though?' she cooed in what sounded very much like a London accent. Her teeth were incongruously strong and bright white in her raddled, ancient face. 'I bet them lot were planning on doing awful, awful things to her.' She smiled very kindly, and Rose couldn't help smiling back. 'Don't you worry, my pet, everything's all right now. We're normal.'

One of the big, bearded men from the raiding party, who looked about thirty, was standing next to her, the stone drinking vessel in his hand. 'I wonder where she's from, Mum,' he said slowly. 'I bet she came down from the hill country, that's what I reckon.'

'Oh, and we all want to hear your theories, don't we?' the old woman said scathingly. 'Let the poor girl speak for herself.' She jabbed him in his side with a bony elbow. 'Go and get my shawl. Go on, I'm freezing my bum off out here.'

'Mum,' he protested.

She thwacked him. 'Get!'

He scurried away. His mother sniffed and spat, then turned back to Rose. 'Are you from over the hills, my dear?'

Rose decided to tell the truth as best she could. 'Yeah. Up there, up nearer the river.'

'Ooh,' said the old woman, surprised. 'River People? You don't look like one. What's your name, then?'

Rose remembered that handshakes seemed to be acknowledged in this time and offered her hand. 'I'm

Rose. Rose Tyler.'

The old woman gave her a big hug. 'You poor thing, Rose of the Tylers.'

'No, not Rose of the Tylers, just Rose Tyler.'

The old woman scrunched up her eyes. 'What's a tyler, then?'

Rose struggled for an answer. 'It's just my surname, doesn't mean anything.'

'All names mean something,' said the old woman. She gave Rose another drink from the cup. 'Did they treat you bad? They're an evil lot, Them.'

Rose felt a surge of anger as the memory of the raid returned to her. 'They're not, they're just people who look a bit different.'

'No, no.' The old woman shook her head and said in a gently patronising tone, 'They're devils.'

'They call you – they call us – Them,' said Rose.

'I'm sure they do, love, but they actually are Them, you see. Did you get a good look? They're not normal, are they?'

Rose flushed, remembering the casual racism of some of her own grandmother's friends back home. 'Why did you attack them?'

'Why?' The old woman sighed. 'You can't have Them where you come from, otherwise you'd know.'

Rose decided to give up for the moment. As with her nan's bingo mates, there was no point arguing about it. She decided to risk moving her still woozy head to get a proper look round.

She was in a more hilly area, still overgrown but much more open. A broad, clear stream came downhill about half a mile away and several fishermen sat on its banks, spears outstretched. There was a fire much like the one in the Neanderthal camp and gathered round it were many more of this tribe. A large group of them looked as if they were playing some sort of game, rolling a stone onto the flattened grass between them and making the same kind of sounds of mock-elation and mock-despair you might hear from a family playing Pictionary. Others – mostly the women – were working on spears or putting together handfuls of berries and greens obviously gathered from the forest. Other women were carrying great bundles of fish wrapped up in rushes. Some men were working on spear-making. But these spears, Rose noticed, were longer and were made from yew or some other bendy wood, and the men's movements were more fluid and gracious than those of the Neanderthal spear-makers. The men chatted to each other good-humouredly. Behind this large open area was the wide entrance to a cave, with people drifting in and out. The general atmosphere was relaxed, almost cosy. Rose found that hard to square with the savage behaviour of these people on their raid.

She realised that the old woman was stroking her hair between her fingers. 'Your Tylers, did they send you down here on your own? That's madness, young girl on her own.' She tutted. 'Sent to trade, were you? Ain't got much on you. They must've stolen it if you had. Did they?'

Rose struggled to reply. 'I'm only following about half of this,' she said honestly.

'Well, your lot, River People, you only come down here when you've got something to trade for our flint,' the old woman continued. 'Ain't you got nothing?'

Rose was worried about the note of suspicion creeping into the woman's voice. 'Yeah, I came to trade, of course,' she lied, immediately wishing she hadn't.

The old woman reached casually inside Rose's pocket. 'What you got, then?' She pulled out Rose's mobile phone, a nail file and a handful of loose change. 'Pretty necklace.' She flipped open the phone and frowned at its mini-screen uncomprehendingly, then handed it back. 'Got a skill, then? Come on!'

Rose searched her mind desperately. A skill. What skill did she have that would be of use to these people? She looked down at her perfectly manicured nails. Of course...

She'd seen her mum do it millions of times. And it was something that never seemed to have occurred to these people. So she thought she'd give it a go.

When Rose had finished filing, the old woman held up her manicured hands to the crowd of tribespeople that had gathered round her. 'She's done 'em lovely! Look! Ain't she clever?'

There was a swelling roar of appreciation from the tribe, male and female alike, and cries of 'Me next!' and 'Can I go after you?' and 'I asked first!'

Rose coughed and raised her voice. 'OK, form a queue!'

'What's a queue?' asked a woman.

'I've just invented it,' said Rose proudly. 'Stand in a line and wait your turn!'

The Doctor was a happy man.

He woke feeling serene. His thoughts were ordered and calm, one flowing into the next logically. He couldn't help smiling, and it was not his normal wonky grin but a reaction to his feeling of utter contentment, with himself and with the universe around him. The usual background noise of worry, excitement and head-buzzing ideas was gone, and he felt deeply satisfied down to the soles of his boots. That was very wrong, but he found that he didn't seem to mind.

'Hello,' said a warm, caring voice. 'And how do you feel?'

The Doctor looked up at Chantal. He couldn't work out why he hadn't noticed her outstanding beauty and charisma before. 'I feel fine,' he told her. 'No, I feel really good. Really, really good.'

'That's lovely,' said Chantal. 'No wrong-feeling at all?'

The Doctor realised he was lying back on some kind of comfy seat, something like a padded dentist's chair.

'None,' said the Doctor. He tried to remember, but the effort was too much and there was no point in it anyway. 'I was… really steamed up about something.' The thought popped into his head. 'Oh yeah, those monsters you're breeding. Hy-Bractors.'

Chantal laughed and stroked the back of her hand against his cheek. 'No need to worry about them. What's the point in worrying about anything?'

The Doctor saw the wisdom in those words. He knew he had been a very anxious person, running around getting concerned about things. And it hadn't made him feel good, not like he did now.

Rose was filing away at the nails of the old woman's son, whose name was Gual. As she used the curved end of the file to pick out huge lumps of grit and dirt from under his nails, she threw a glance at the game players by the fire and decided to risk asking a question that had been bothering her.

'Shouldn't you lot be out hunting or something?'

'I've done my week's work, don't you worry,' said Gual, sounding slightly affronted. 'I do Mondays, Tuesdays and Thursdays.'

'You do a three-day week?' asked Rose.

'It's Wednesday, and I got Wednesday off, ain't I?' said Gual.

The old woman lurched back over. 'And even when he's working he messes about while everyone else puts in their hand's turn. He's a useless lump, Rose.' She tapped him on the shoulder, hard. 'Good job we got some proper men in this tribe, innit?'

'Mum, will you give it a rest?' said Gual ineffectually.

His mother pushed him aside roughly and sat herself down in front of Rose. 'You got my bone?' she told her son. 'Go and get my bone. I'm starving here and there's some lovely marrow on that.'

Gual mumbled and slouched off towards the cave entrance.

'And fetch the apron of Ghelthath while you're

about it!' The old woman turned back to Rose. 'He ain't such a bad lad,' the old woman sighed, 'but a severe disappointment to me. You should have seen his father. Ooh, he was like one of the Ancestors reborn. Lovely big shoulders, threw a spear easy as clicking his fingers.'

'I've already done you,' Rose pointed out, indicating the old woman's immaculately filed nails.

'No, Rose, I just came over for more of our chat,' said the old woman. 'You got a husband back home, have you, dear?'

'No,' said Rose.

'Really? I say. Not engaged?'

'Was once, but it didn't work out.'

The old woman shook her head sadly. 'Got eaten by something, did he?'

'I hope so,' said Rose.

'So you're free and single, are ya? Let me have a look at you, love. Stand up a second.'

Rose obeyed. Her plan at the moment was to ingratiate herself with these people and then slip out after nightfall and make her way back to Osterberg. That was slightly complicated by the fact that she had no idea where she'd been taken to, and there were no landmarks here that she recognised. But it was a good enough plan to be going on with.

The old woman gave her a thorough look-over, turning her about, sizing her up from head to toe with almost hungry eyes. Rose had a momentary flash of fear – they couldn't be cannibals, could they?

'Look at your lovely figure. Hips a bit of a problem,

I suppose, very thin, but I think you'll do.'

'Do for what?' asked Rose, tensing up with an anxious look at the fire.

The old woman gave her another big, and surprisingly powerful, squeeze. 'You're a very lucky girl, Rose Tyler. What a polite young lady you are.'

'I won't be if you don't tell me what you're talking about,' said Rose.

'We've had a chat back in the cave, me and the other old girls, and –' she paused and seemed to stifle a tear – 'we've decided you're going to join the Family!' She made the announcement with great pride and Rose realised from the old woman's tone that this was some kind of great honour. But she couldn't bring herself to react with the joy that it was clearly designed to inspire.

'OK,' she said slowly. 'What exactly do you mean there?'

'Oh, come here,' said the old woman, holding her even tighter. 'Look how happy you've made me, Rose. I'm welling up here. I'm gonna think of you as my daughter.'

'Right, adoption,' said Rose. 'That's really kind, thanks.'

'I know why they sent you down here, the Tylers,' the old woman went on. 'Young girl sent out on her own, not hard to see why.'

'Yeah, to use my skills,' said Rose, trying to keep up.

'And the rest,' said the old woman. 'You're a gift to us. We'll be allied to the Tylers, our flint for your… what is it again?'

'Manicuring,' said Rose.

She was beginning to work it out. The scattered human tribes must use trade partnerships to form alliances. She decided to encourage the old woman. The more they accepted her, the less likely they were to keep their eye on her too closely, and then she could be away.

'Yeah, I'm really glad to be one of the Family, er…'

'Call me Nan,' said the old woman.

'Nan,' said Rose happily. 'Shall I get on with my work?'

'No. What are you like? You haven't met him yet, have you?' said Nan.

'Met who?'

Nan sighed. 'My lovely grandson.'

'And why would I need to meet him?' asked Rose, worries rising again.

'Well, you wanna give the goods a look-over, don'tcha?' said Nan. 'You wanna see what you're gonna be marrying.'

Rose gulped. 'Marrying?'

'Yes, you're gonna marry him, love,' said Nan. 'It'll be lovely, and we'll have good Tyler blood and lots of pretty Tyler babies in the Family, make us strong.'

'I'm not,' said Rose simply.

'You are!' Nan shouted gleefully. 'I know you can't believe your luck!'

'No, I'm really not,' said Rose firmly.

'You're too modest,' said Nan. 'Lovely girl like you was made to be queen. We'll have it all done by tonight, and then a grand fish supper!'

Rose coughed. 'Thanks, Nan, but where I come from, right, it's not decided like this. Like, I have a say in it, and there's loads to sort out – takes months – order of service, seating plan, are the invites gonna be plain or embossed…' She realised she was babbling.

'Here he is now!' said Nan proudly.

'OK, I'm flattered, but I am not getting married to some big hairy cave person,' said Rose very definitely.

And then she saw Nan's grandson walking towards her, and he was probably the fittest boy she had ever seen.

'On the other hand, though…' said Rose.

NINE

The Doctor could tell Chantal was doing something to him, but he didn't care what it was. He had no interest in anything but lying here and looking up out of the metal chair at the light that hung from the ceiling of the small wooden room. Even the ceiling wasn't that interesting, but then what did being interested get you? A lot of stress, he seemed to recall, though right at the moment stress just sounded like a word for a feeling it was impossible to think he would ever experience again.

'By the way, where do you come from?' asked Chantal, leaning over him.

The Doctor was happy to answer her. If there was anything he could do to please Chantal, he'd do it. 'I'm an alien, from a planet you'll never have heard of. It got blown up at the end of a war. I'm usually bothered about that, but now...' He grinned. 'I don't care.' He gave a deep sigh. 'That's... nice.'

'Of course it is,' said Chantal. 'And did you come to Earth in a space rocket?'

'No,' said the Doctor breezily. He knew he'd always been tight-lipped about personal details in the past, but he couldn't remember why, so he went on, 'No, well, sort of. It's called the TARDIS, Time And Relative Dimension In Space. It can travel anywhere, anywhen. I came back here to have a look at what you lot are up to with your primitive time engine, cos it's quite dangerous. There was a Neanderthal man running round the twenty-first century, you know!'

'Yes, that was unfortunate,' said Chantal. 'He found his way into the town, went wild, but I got rid of him before he could do any damage. Popped him into the time beam and packed him off somewhere at random. Anyway, don't fret, because we won't be using it again. Is it really that primitive?'

'Laughably,' said the Doctor.

'It would be nice to see your TARDIS, if it's so much better,' said Chantal.

'Oh, right, you're welcome. I'll show you round, full guided tour. Shouldn't take longer than a couple of years.'

Chantal carried on doing whatever she was doing. The Doctor was vaguely aware of a numbness in every part of his body from the neck down and a kind of squelching sound.

'Knew you were lying when you turned up,' she said, 'but I thought I'd see what you got up to before I intervened.'

'I'm really sorry if I did anything wrong,' said the Doctor, feeling a distant pang of disquiet at the thought he might have somehow displeased Chantal.

'Don't worry,' said Chantal. 'Interesting that you're not human. Though I worked it out before you told me.'

'Ah, what gave me away?' asked the Doctor, sensing that she wanted to tell him.

'Your blood for a start,' said Chantal, holding up a thin glass tube containing a sample. 'It's very different from human blood, and full of acids that I've never seen before. You'll have to tell me what they're all for.'

'OK,' said the Doctor. 'Well, I've got a self-regenerating genetic imprimatur that –'

'Not now,' said Chantal. She looked into the blood in the tube. 'I had to really up the dose on your popper pack to make sure it would get past your defences. Now you've got a massive dose of general well-being flooding into your brain, which I'm also curious about.'

'I can tell you all about my brain too,' said the Doctor. 'Later?'

'Later.' Chantal put the tube down and said, 'Your heart's beating very slowly, though, Doctor.'

The Doctor raised an eyebrow. 'Oh yeah? Which one?'

'This one, the right,' Chantal replied, and she held it up, a big red throbbing meaty lump, for him to see.

He realised that Chantal had opened up his chest and was poking around in it, taking bits out and putting bits in. And something inside him, buried away in a dark corner of his mind, didn't like the idea.

Chantal indicated another thing. 'The design is rather fascinating. The intriguing monotony in the occurrence of inter-caval conduction block during typical atrial flutter suggests an anatomic or electrophysiological predisposition for conduction abnormalities.'

The Doctor said nothing. The wrong-feeling stirred again.

The people in Osterberg were designed to be attractive, thought Rose, and she'd rather shallowly been slightly taken with that at first. But the boy-band artificiality of Jacob or Reddy was thrown into sharp contrast by the looks of her prospective husband. He had one of those wonky, asymmetrical faces that you could stare at for ages. He managed to look rough and pretty at the same time, and even with a straggly beard that was half bum fluff, a face splattered with badly applied woad and dressed in a kind of smelly leather skirt he still managed to look like the boy next door combined with the boy who was too beautiful to live.

Nan and the others had backed off to allow Rose and the boy – who was called Tillun – to get to know each other. Rose struggled to make conversation, and, she was pleased to see, so did Tillun. He was fit but didn't know it, which made him even more fit. To fill the silence, Rose asked about the game with the stone, which was still being played by an avid crowd of tribespeople of all ages.

'But everyone plays crakkits, don't they?' asked Tillun, flicking his super-kissable floppy hair.

'No, never heard of it, honest,' said Rose.

'What do they play up the river, then?' asked Tillun.

'Plenty of games, but it's all really different,' Rose replied. She decided to try and broach the really important subject. Stunning as Tillun was, she still had to get out of this madness and back to the Doctor. 'We don't get married so quick either.'

Tillun grunted, as if her opinion didn't count for much. 'Well, maybe that's your custom. But you're here with us now, aren't you? So you can follow ours.' He smiled at her, exposing another set of strong, gleaming white teeth. 'Nan's done me proud. I quite fancied Jarul over there, but you're in another league.'

Rose frowned. 'And my input into this decision would be zero, right?'

She wasn't getting through to him. 'My nan's the wise woman,' he said, as if it was the answer to everything.

'My nan's pretty sharp too,' ventured Rose. 'And what she'd say if she was here is "wait a while, see how you both get on". She got married too quick and it was a disaster. He was carrying on with half the other women in the… tribe, behind her back.'

'That's terrible,' said Tillun. He reached out a comforting hand to her shoulder and Rose could hardly stop him.

'Yeah, see, so why not wait a while?'

Tillun said sincerely and pleasantly, without a trace of machismo or ego, 'We'll have no secrets in our marriage. When I carry on with other women, Rose, I promise I will do it right in front of you.'

Nan reappeared. 'You all set, lovebirds? We'll get started about three.' She indicated a stone marker, some kind of megalith, at the top of a nearby hill. 'Just when the sun hits the stone of the goddess Brelalla.'

She threw a big furry pelt at Rose. It felt rough and

well worn, but it had clearly been very well looked after. 'There you go, Rose. I wore that, ooh, must be thirty years ago now.' She handed her a random collection of sorry-looking daffodils and bluebells arranged in a bunch of tied-together twigs. 'And there's your corsage. Stand up. Let's have a look at you.'

Rose got to her feet, modelling the 'wedding dress' and flowers.

Nan nudged her grandson. 'Don't she look lovely?'

'Soon have you all back together,' said Chantal. She waved a pencil laser, not totally unlike the sonic screwdriver in design, over the Doctor's chest. There was no pain, not even any blood, no hint of a scar. 'Then we can go and look at your TARDIS.'

'Which you think can take you off to deliver value through all time and space,' said the Doctor.

He could feel a trace of some incompatible emotion struggling to break out, though he couldn't yet put a name to it.

'I detect a hint of sarcasm,' said Chantal. 'Better remedy that.' She leaned over him and tapped a number into the popper pack that she had attached on his left side. 'There.'

'I see. You've found the part of the brain that controls sarcasm, have you?' said the Doctor. 'Very clever.'

'Sorry, was that sarcastic?' said Chantal, frowning slightly.

The Doctor paused, unsure. He felt the power to be sarcastic melt away as the chemicals did their work.

'It was,' he admitted. 'But no, actually, it is very

clever. I mean that.'

'Good,' said Chantal. 'Yes, I've always wanted to go into space. I know people did once, long ago. Earth had an empire that reached deep into the stars. You can give me the secret.'

She sat the Doctor up and helped him back into his sweater and jacket. As he moved, he felt a tinge of nausea wash over him, and it was as if the thoughts that had been pushed away by the great serenity he'd felt were loosened up and shaken back out into his brain like a bag of nails. He felt his personality, what made him *him* and not just a collection of electrical impulses, his Doctorness, heading back towards him, as if it was trying to step back inside him and reassert itself. An overwhelming urge to ask a question...

'Why are you doing... whatever you're doing?' he heard himself say. 'Why are you breeding those things, the Hy-Bractors?'

'They're not things, they're people,' said Chantal. 'Technically speaking, as human as me and you – well, me.'

The Doctor's gaze focused on Chantal's popper pack and another question filled the void left by the first. 'If you are on these drugs... where are you getting your ideas from? Cos I'm usually full of ideas and I'm not getting any, and it's a weird feeling and I don't like it.'

Chantal leaned over and pressed more buttons on his pack. 'Forget about that.'

'Cos, if I was thinking like I normally think, I'd be thinking of...'

'Just relax,' said Chantal.

The Doctor felt thoughts tumbling slowly towards him. 'I'd be thinking of… a way to… an idea… It's nearly there, I've nearly got it… Cos if you can have ideas, I can have ideas… All I want is one, come on, idea… I know you're in there… Come on, baby, you can do it… You're trying so hard, come on, work those neurones, kid…'

Chantal looked on, amused. 'You'll never do it.'

The Doctor blinked. 'Oh, that is so obvious,' he said.

'What?' asked Chantal.

'This,' said the Doctor, and he leaped at her, grabbing her arms behind her back and pinning her against a wall.

Then they just stood there as he tried to have another idea.

Chantal raised an eyebrow. Her face was very close to the Doctor's; he could feel her fragrant breath.

'And what are you gonna do now? Kiss me?'

The Doctor considered. 'That's an idea.' He frowned. 'But not the one I want right this second! How about this?'

He hauled her over to the chair and laid her down on it, at the same time reaching for a long coil of wire on a nearby trolley that was littered with surgical tools. Quickly he looped the wire around her body and the chair.

'Oh, they're coming out now… and I'm putting my hand in my pocket for some reason…' He gripped the sonic screwdriver and its reassuring shape and solidity sent a fresh wave of ingenuity through him. He looked at it for a second. 'Oh, it's this…' A couple of seconds passed as he tried to work out what he could do with it. 'Right, got it!' he cried exultantly, and switching it to a particularly arcane setting he welded the loops of wire to the chair, trapping Chantal.

'Ingenious,' she said, seemingly unconcerned. 'I can't wait to take a look at your brain. It must have all sorts of defences I didn't know about.'

The Doctor tried to formulate a witty reply, but this power was lost to him. So he just said, 'Tough titty!', waved his finger ineffectually and walked out of Chantal's examination room.

He emerged onto the main street of Osterberg and started clicking his fingers anxiously. 'Come on!' He stared about blankly. 'One useful thought every thirty seconds, that's rubbish,' he said despairingly. 'Come on…' He banged his hands against his brows aggressively, treating it like an old TV set, and the thought of an old TV set triggered a thought of…

'Quilley! Find Quilley!'

After another thirty seconds remembering who Quilley was, why he was important and where he might be, he raced off.

The Doctor burst into Quilley's hut. Quilley was going over some work notes at the table. He looked up and smiled. 'Hello, Doctor.'

The Doctor smiled back. 'Found you. Great.' He walked over and gave Quilley a pat on the shoulder. 'But was that it?'

'Anything I can do for you in particular?' asked Quilley.

The Doctor thought. 'Nope.' His eye was caught by Quilley's old settee. 'That looks comfy.' He sat down and shuffled about. 'This is in fact the comfiest cushion in the universe.'

'Thanks.'

The Doctor drummed his fingers idly. 'That was all I had to do today, I reckon.' He stretched out on the settee and yawned. 'Nap ahoy.'

Just as his eyelids were descending, he caught sight of something stuffed into the ancient washing machine in the corner. It was a long blue coat and it made him sit up again. 'Rose. Something about Rose...'

'Rose is nice,' put in Quilley.

'Yeah,' said the Doctor. 'I like Rose. I like Rose... Rose... yeah, but I like Rose...'

He shuddered as a series of images flashed through his mind – *Rose smiling. Rose taking his hand. Rose in danger.*

'Whoah, what was that? There was something else... Find Rose.' A surge of glee possessed him. '*Escape and find Rose!* Come on!'

He leaped from the settee and grabbed Rose's coat, tying it round himself as an *aide-mémoire*, then jostled Quilley out of the door. 'Oh yeah, you won't need that!' he cried, grabbing the popper pack marked TERRY on Quilley's chest and ripping it off. 'And neither will I.' He ripped his own off.

They hurried back into the street.

'Where are we going?' asked Quilley mildly.

'Good point,' said the Doctor, drawing to a halt. He patted Rose's coat. 'What would Rose do? Come on…' He clenched his fists and he saw Rose saying…

'Antidote!'

A few minutes later they were standing in the town's supply centre, one wall of the shack taken up by a wooden rack containing refills for the popper packs. The Doctor searched along the labelled columns of drugs.

'Gotta be an antidote. Something I can use…' He stopped and turned slowly to Quilley. 'Hold on a sec. This project – it was supposed to last forty days and you've been here forty-nine, yeah?'

'Yes,' said Quilley.

He remained dazed and acquiescent, though the effects of the popper pack were fading a bit, and a little of the pomp and fire was returning to his face.

The Doctor roughly pulled the rack away from the wall and shook the contents out. There were only about five or six refills left.

'Then you've run out,' said the Doctor. 'Used it all up. Pretty soon this'll be a dry town. Everyone's gonna be normal.'

'Oh.' Quilley blinked. 'Isn't that a good thing?'

Chantal waited patiently, strapped to the chair, for the Osterbergers to come looking for her. She knew they would. They were only interested in pleasing her, after all.

The zoo-tech called Tom popped his head round

the door of her examination room. 'What are you doing there, Chantal?' he asked.

'None of your business,' she said politely. 'Untie me. Use the cutter on the trolley.'

Tom walked over. Chantal noted the unusual expression on his face. He was registering disquiet. Instinctively he reached up and dialled a reassuring combo into himself, but the disquiet remained. He wouldn't know the popper pack was nearly empty. It was Chantal's concern to supply refills and as there were almost none left she'd stopped doing it. It didn't matter any more, anyway, not now the Hy-Bractors were about to emerge.

Tom picked up the cutter, switched it on and hesitated. 'I've got a wrong-feeling about this,' he said. 'I've got a wrong-feeling about you, Chantal.'

'The sooner you release me, the sooner I can stop the wrong-feeling,' Chantal pointed out.

That sounded reasonable to Tom, so he cut carefully through the coils of wire.

Chantal sprang to her feet, adjusted her suit and took him by the arm. 'Let's go and sort it all out,' she said.

Chantal led Tom to the Grey Door. 'Just stand there, darling,' she told him, positioning him right opposite it.

'I don't want to,' said Tom, looking anxiously over at the skeleton on the floor a few feet away.

'I've got a surprise, to stop the wrong-feeling,' Chantal reassured him. She knocked on the Grey

Door and called 'X01! It's Chantal!'

The Grey Door swung slowly open.

'Yes. What?' said a rasping voice. 'Is there more food?'

'I've had to bring things forward,' Chantal called in. 'There's an alien here, the one you spoke to, and potentially he could mess things up. Now I know you're not quite ready, but I'm sure you're up to it. Come on.'

'But is there food?' said the voice.

'I'll show you.'

The first Hy-Bractor lunged out from the Grey Door, its tail flicking rapidly about.

Tom screamed. He couldn't move for the sheer amounts of wrong-feeling pumping through him.

The Hy-Bractor blinked and pointed at him. 'Are you human?'

'Yes, he is,' said Chantal. 'Get it?'

'And can I eat him, Chantal?' asked the Hy-Bractor.

'No,' blurted Tom.

'Yes,' said Chantal.

As Tom started to run, the Hy-Bractor lunged, grabbing him round the waist in its massive lumpy grey hand. Then it tore his arm off and munched on it thoughtfully. 'The humans are inferior, you're right,' it said through chomping, bloody mouthfuls.

'As I told you,' said Chantal, 'I'm always right.' She rapped harshly on the door. 'Come on, all of you, out! Time to deliver! Time to inherit the Earth!'

Week 3
Das's Journal

This was the week I began to understand something very important. Humans do a thing called lying. It's a kind of deliberate mistake. I'll try to explain.

One night, Jack told me that there weren't any crisps left in our cupboard. But later on I went to the cupboard for some jaffa cakes and I saw that there was a family bag of assorted crisps. I told Jack he'd been mistaken, but he got slightly angry. He said he'd told me there were no crisps even though he knew we still had some, because I was eating badly and he was trying to stop me eating badly.

I tried to hold the thought in my mind. It took me a few goes. A lie is when a human doesn't want another human to know the truth and instead makes them think a mistake is true. Jack says I will be able to grasp it if I keep thinking about it. To help me, he told me about something called quantum physics. Apparently, humans don't understand that a thing changes when you're looking at it, which is obvious. They have to really think to make it clear in their heads until they accept it, the idiots. And the same holds for me and lying.

To help me out, Jack made me tell a few lies. I told him he had fair hair and he was a woman. It's quite easy. I got the hang of it quickly enough. Of course, the trouble now is that Jack thinks he has fair hair and is a woman because of my lies. I'll tell him the truth soon, but it's funny to think my lies have fooled him. Funny is something else I am just discovering. It means you know something other people don't. It isn't really cruel, because everybody here has so much stuff they don't need to be so loyal to each other any longer.

I've realised a lot of the tribes on television are liars. Footballers and news and Trisha are telling the truth, but nearly everybody else is pretending, to amuse people. I was very relieved to discover this. People laugh at the Grace Brothers, for example, because they know they are liars.

It was important to learn about lying, because this week I went out and had some job interviews. I need to work so that I will get money to spend on food. Jack told me about different tribes I could join and I decided building was the best. I went to a building site and lied to a man that I was from Romania and that I had worked on building sites before. I start next Monday. It'll be nice to have something to do and everybody there seems very friendly. And I can laugh at them because I know something they don't.

One night we went to a nightclub in London, which Bromley is only a part of. Instead of cola, Jack and I bought cans of beer. You have to be very careful with beer because it brings you closer to the happiness of the gods, and if you drink too much the gods resent it and punish you with head pain. So I only had two all night. It made me realise that some human females can be very attractive, and Jack told me to go for it and woo them.

I wooed a very nice woman – she wasn't very pretty, far too thin, but she spoke of many strange and wise things, and warned me of wasps. Jack didn't like her and steered me away from her. He said it was for my own good and there would be too many complications. She did seem to be a very complicated person.

Later on we were queuing up for a taxi to go home and we got talking to some women who liked Jack a lot. (That's funny, because of course at the moment he thinks he himself is a woman, thanks to my lie!) One of the girls was rather left out. I don't understand why, as she was by far the prettiest. She is short, has the fat of a good hunter and a lovely big nose, and even some hair on her cheeks and mouth. She smells of sweat and the forest. She doesn't laugh as much as other humans either, which is a relief. Her name is Anna Marie – her friends call her Big Fat Anna Marie No-Mates, as they revere her – and she gave me her telephone number. I'm looking forward to seeing her again and starting my job.

I love this world of plenty and boredom.

Captain Jack Harkness's Data-Record

I've finally got through to Das about lying. I reckoned that it was a concept he could imitate, even if he never quite understands it.

It reminds me of when I tried, a few years back, to sell tickets to watch the horse racing in second-century Rome to a party of humanoid Cephalids. Cephalids are the most notorious gamblers in space and love sporting occasions on their own planet. But they evolved so they can see the universe in nine dimensions simultaneously, so the kinds of sport they play at home are weird events like the Ratio Acceleration Derby and Atom-Boarding. To us three-dimensional folks, that just looks like staring at an accretion of invisible gas particles for seven years, but boy do they get worked up about it – and the money that changes hands is off the scale. I knew I had to lift some of that, so I took some back to the Circus Maximus and drew up a slate.

But to the Cephalids the horse race must have looked as weird and boring as Atom-Boarding did to me. It was a big letdown for them, but not for me.

My slate was so baffling to them they paid up millions right away out of embarrassment. Anyhow, a year later they realised what I'd done and sent a battle cruiser after me. But being Cephalids, their lame multi-dimensional weapons kept firing at where I'd been and where I was gonna be or where I might have decided to go in some kooky alternative universe rather than where I actually was.

The point of that little tale is that eventually the Cephalids got it – they unravelled a concept, horse racing, that was completely alien. And I figured that Das, who is nearer to Homo sapiens than the Cephalids ever were, would get lying and fiction if I really spelled it out to him. And he's gonna need a bit of evasion if he's gotta stay here.

And I think I've cracked it. Took him through slow, step by step. Das has sure taken to lying. He went for a job interview at a building site and walked it. So I'm feeling proud of my boy right now.

I had to do some lying of my own on our night out. We went uptown a little and Das got talking to a pretty cute older woman – I listened in on my Wrist-o-Matic to make sure he was coping. 'Wasps will dive-bomb certain brands of hairspray,' she was saying in an accent just like Rose's. God knows how the conversation had ended up there. 'And bright colours. I was wearing a vivid lemon gilet and had my hair up to here and I got three stings in a day. I was like a wasp magnet.'

Something about that voice, something about her face, sounded too familiar. I ran a quick microgenetic check and the Wrist-o-Matic flashed up a close correspondence. She was only Rose's mother. So I grabbed Das and got him out of there. There's just too much synchronicity in the universe as it is, and from what I hear she's not the kind of woman who'd appreciate any more Doctor-related weirdness in her life. I told Das she was part of a warrior tribe he should keep away from.

But later on in the taxi queue he struck lucky anyway. If there is any trace of Neanderthal genes left in the human race, well, he found it all right.

TEN

'We've got this tradition in my tribe, the Tylers, right?' said Rose, shivering in her flimsy wedding skins. 'Before she gets married, a girl has to walk out and face the sun alone, to appease the mighty god… Ooh-la-la. If we don't, then the god will take away the hunting and dry up the river.'

She hoped she sounded more convincing to Nan and Gual than she sounded to herself.

'That sounds sensible,' said Nan. 'You'd better go and do it. We don't want some goddess we ain't never heard of punishing us, do we? Our own ones are tough enough to please. I'll come and keep you company.'

'No, sorry, Nan. I have to do it on my own,' said Rose.

'Why?' asked Gual suspiciously.

'It's part of the Tylers' holy ritual,' said Rose.

She glanced anxiously over at the cave entrance. Tillun was in there now, being prepared. She was pretty sure he wouldn't swallow her unlikely story.

Nan waved her off. 'Don't take too long about it. It's a quarter past two.' She told the time by looking at the sun's position in the sky. 'Though we'll never be ready at this rate.' She turned to her son. 'Who's had the Great Fish of Matrimony?'

'I'm going to get it in a minute,' said Gual through gritted teeth, in the tone of voice people reserve for members of their family.

'Well, go and get it now!' Nan shot back in much the same way.

Rose did her best to saunter out of the camp, without looking back.

The workers in the observation room were beginning to feel a bit strange anyway and were waiting for Chantal to come and put them right. None of them wanted to be the first to say anything about the worried, sweaty way they were feeling, but the haunted looks they gave each other and the anxious atmosphere were building up. The tiny non-verbal signals made by humans, suppressed from birth in these people, were returning to them.

They realised something was definitely wrong when the door of the room crashed open to reveal four Hy-Bractors. The first was the one encountered by the Doctor and Quilley, the remains of Tom dribbling from its heavy-jawed mouth. The others were another male and a female, all dressed in sharp business suits, their tails flicking over their heads.

To the humans the Hy-Bractors were practically indistinguishable. To the Hy-Bractors the humans were practically indistinguishable.

'Are you humans?' asked the female, sniffing.

'Of course they are!' snapped the first male.

They advanced into the observation room, and then there was a lot of screaming and eating.

In the storage room the Doctor heard that screaming and cursed his fuzzy head. He had almost beaten off the massive amounts of drugs Chantal had pumped into his body, but it was still hard to think quickly. And every half a minute a wave of some relaxant passed over his muscles, making him long to ignore everything and just find a place to take a seat and chill the day away.

'OK, right, focus,' he said. 'Let's have some focus.'

There were more screams.

'Quilley, we've gotta move everyone out of here. Are you getting that?'

Quilley was slumped against the wall, staring off into space. 'What's the big panic? Can I just lie down for a second?' He started to slump towards the floor.

The Doctor, galvanised, hauled him to his feet and almost spat in his face with sudden purpose. 'No! Listen!' He shook Quilley as the screams echoed round the caves. 'Those creatures behind the Grey Door, Hy-Bractors, I don't know why, or what they are, but they're gonna kill everybody, and the people here will go meekly to their deaths like lambs for Chantal because they're not like you and me! Quilley!'

'I can tell you're very worked up about it,' said Quilley, 'and yeah, I respect you for feeling that way, but does it matter?'

'They'll kill you!' shouted the Doctor, staring right into his eyes. 'Reach inside yourself. Come on, T. P.

Quilley, the Refuser! The man who turned to this brave new world and said no! I need you!'

'You're trying to make me feel wrong,' said Quilley, brushing him off. 'And do you mind not spitting on my collar?'

'I'm irritating you. Something's stirring. Great!' said the Doctor. 'Right, another way to irritate you…' He prodded Quilley in the chest, poked him in the side, turned him round and goosed him for good measure.

'Would you please stop doing that?' Quilley's voice went up a notch, the first hint of his usual barking loudness.

'Stop me! Come on, what'cha gonna do?' The Doctor goaded him like a playground bully, wedging him and giving him a slap.

'Get off!' stormed Quilley, slapping him back.

Their hands met and grasped. There was a silence, punctuated by cries of bewilderment and consternation from outside, still some distance away at the other end of the town.

Then the Doctor slapped Quilley once more.

'I'm back,' fumed Quilley. 'You can stop!'

'You're just saying that!' said the Doctor, prepared to slap again.

'No, you really can stop!' Quilley listened to the sounds drifting over the town. 'Chantal – what's she done? Why?'

'We can work that out later!' cried the Doctor. 'Right now we've gotta save these people!'

There was a rat-a-tat-tat on the door and a voice

called out politely, 'Are you humans?'

'Right after we've saved ourselves,' said the Doctor, backing away.

'Why not try what you did before?' hissed Quilley.

'Won't work now. They're out in the open. They've seen what humans are,' said the Doctor. He picked up the fallen storage cabinet and swung it in front of the door, then set about piling desks and chairs on top of it. 'Help me!' he ordered Quilley.

Quilley swung up a chair as the knocking came again. 'You in there,' said the rasping voice. 'Humans or what?'

'But what is it?' gasped Quilley.

The Doctor ran from the makeshift barricade to the back of the storage room and started to kick at the wooden slats with his boots, trying to knock through a back way out. 'It's a predator,' he gasped. 'There are thirteen and a half million species on this planet at any given moment in its history. Life seeps from the pores of this world. And up until now, you were the ones at the top. You kicked the Neanderthals – this lot are gonna kick you!'

The barricade shifted. 'I'm coming in to check,' said the voice.

Quilley shuddered uncontrollably. 'What can we do?'

'What prey always does,' said the Doctor, kicking the last few slats away.

'Run?' asked Quilley.

'Works for me,' said the Doctor, ducking through the hole just as the barricade behind them toppled over and a Hy-Bractor lurched through. Quilley shot out after him.

They stopped running a few minutes later, when the Doctor felt confident they had evaded their pursuer. He had chosen a deliberately illogical, circuitous escape route in the hope that the Hy-Bractor, which after all was new to the world, would get confused in the higgledy-piggledy streets of the town, and now they were at the foot of the steps leading out.

They stood and watched the Osterbergers. A few of them had come out onto the streets, looking confusedly about, listening to the screams – which had stopped for a minute – and muttering laconically to each other about Chantal doing something to sort whatever it was out.

The Doctor turned to Quilley and looked meaningfully at him. 'You've got to try and do some more bravery.'

Quilley paled. 'What do you mean?'

'We can't stop them,' said the Doctor, 'we can only run away. At least until my mind gets back to normal and I can think of a way to do it. But someone has gotta warn the people up on the surface too, tell them to run. The Neanderthals, the humans. They're my responsibility. These people are yours.'

'And you've got to warn Rose,' said Quilley. 'Because you care for her.'

'And you've gotta care for the people here,' said the Doctor, 'save as many as you can, get them to run. With any luck, the drugs are weakening in their systems. You could stir them up. I know they've never given you anything back, and you've got every reason for hating them and the world you come from, but you've got to try!'

Quilley struck one of his poses. 'Yes, I read about that. Nobility. To dislike a person but to care for their right to live!'

'That's the one,' said the Doctor. 'Do your best, but don't do anything too heroic. There's only a few of them, and they're pretty dumb and slow, but they're just warming up. Simply get as many of your people out of here as you can and then leg it yourself!' He was already bounding up the steps.

Quilley watched him go, then took a deep breath and ran back into the town, calling out desperately, banging on the walls of the huts as he went.

'Listen! Listen to me, you putrid, prostrate idiots! We're getting out of here!'

After slipping away from the cave people, Rose had run up and down the small hills, trying to work out her way to the Neanderthal camp. From there she reckoned she could probably get back to Osterberg, or failing that strike out for the TARDIS. She soon realised her optimism was misplaced. She had no idea where she was heading. There were traces of forest in every direction and nothing to indicate a way back.

She liked to think she'd never panicked in her life. Panic was pointless. But there was a rising sense of fear in the pit of her stomach at the prospect of being out here alone in the wild when darkness fell. She remembered the unseen creature that had menaced her and the Doctor earlier and shuddered. And then there'd be the embarrassment of being mauled to death on the coldest night imaginable while dressed in a fur bikini.

And then she wasn't alone any longer.

A figure emerged from a clump of bushes. Rose tensed – and she realised it was Tillun. He looked downcast.

'I didn't fall for that. We're not stupid down here.'

'Well, at least you're obviously not,' said Rose, suddenly very glad of his company.

'What exactly is wrong with me?' he demanded, coming to stand in front of her.

'Not much,' she had to admit, 'but look, I don't know you.'

'But you'd rather walk out into the forest alone than marry me,' he said sadly. 'Why?'

'Because I met you about two hours ago,' Rose replied.

'But I'm the king,' said Tillun uncomprehendingly. 'The grandson of the wise woman. It's my right.'

In spite of her bizarre surroundings, Rose felt sorry for him. She tried desperately to think of a way to tell him the truth and wondered how to start. 'Where I come from, everyone has the rights of a king,' she said.

Tillun frowned. 'How on earth does that work?'

'Pretty well. We can all do what we like. Nobody tells us what to do.'

'But then how can your tribe survive?' asked Tillun. 'We must all do what's good for the tribe. What we might want for ourselves doesn't matter.'

Rose had met people and aliens with different values on her travels with the Doctor. She remembered talking with Gwyneth in the nineteenth century and how strange that had seemed. Compared to this, it had been easy. It was as if Tillun's brain was wired up differently from hers. Concepts she had lived her life accepting as totally natural were just not there in his language or understanding.

Before she could continue, the sound of galloping hoofs echoed around the plain.

'Down!' hissed Tillun, grabbing her and heaving her into the concealing bushes.

The hoofbeats came closer and then, only feet away from them, stopped. Rose clung onto Tillun, her face pressed close against his beating heart. Something seemed to be moving just a few inches away from them...

The bushes parted. Rose opened her eyes, prepared to face anything.

The Doctor was staring down at her and Tillun, huddled together in the bush. He raised an eyebrow. 'Fast worker,' he said at last.

Rose got up and brushed herself down. 'I'm so glad to see you I'm filing away my reply.'

The Doctor looked her up and down. 'Just the thing for a night out in the Ice Age.'

'This is like Julien McDonald round here,' said Rose.

'You'll get fleas,' said the Doctor.

'I've already got fleas,' said Rose with feeling.

The Doctor nodded across at Tillun, who was just

getting up. 'Who's the new boyf, then?' He shook Tillun's hand. 'Not bad. Like the woad, Aladdin Sane.'

'Actually, I'm her fiancé,' said Tillun, a little aggressively. 'Who are you?'

The Doctor's face was a picture. Then he nodded. 'OK. Lots to talk about… but lots more to do! Get on my horse!' He pointed to where a horse stood placidly a few feet away.

Chantal stood in the observation room, the four Hy-Bractors gathered round her in an attentive circle. The room was littered with the picked-clean skeletons of the staff. After gorging themselves on the meat, the Hy-Bractors had considerately sat them back up in their work chairs.

'OK, not bad,' said Chantal. 'Considering I didn't have time to run the final tests. But we can work round it – it's just a teensy setback. We're going to deliver on this. Got it?' She spoke softly and slowly. 'Kill all humans.'

The leading male put his hand up. 'Chantal?'

'Yes?'

'How do we know if they're humans?'

Chantal grabbed a piece of paper, took a pen from her breast pocket and drew a quick sketch. 'They are all humans,' she said. 'All the talking ones. Except for him in the leather jacket.' She held up the paper, where she had drawn the Doctor with incredible accuracy. 'Do you understand it now? Kill everybody, except each other, and except him, and except me. Don't bother to ask if someone's human or not, you can just work it out for yourselves. I'm not always going to be there for you, am I? And so you've got to learn. OK, your brains are still forming, but you can understand this, can't you?' She sighed. 'So. What are you going to do?'

'Kill all humans?' said the female.

'That's it, there you go,' said Chantal encouragingly.

'We have all got to get out of here!' thundered Quilley.

He was standing in front of a bemused crowd of about thirty Osterbergers who had gathered in the main street in response to his calls. He could tell they were beginning to lose the effects of the popper drugs, but they still retained their sheep-like faith in Chantal thanks to the implanted interest patches in their brains.

'This is just mad Refuser talk,' said Jacob, at the front of the crowd. His arm was around his wife.

'But my wrong-feeling's not going away,' said Lene.

'The packs must be running out. We'll ask Chantal to get us new ones and then we'll be fine.'

'Chantal is insane!' raged Quilley, throwing his arms about. He pointed to her popper pack. 'And that can't help you any longer – there are no popper drugs left! Think about it – you had supplies for forty days, this is day forty-nine! Just do the numbers!'

A wondering silence fell over the crowd. Then Lene swooned. Jacob held her close to him and kissed her forehead. At the same moment a long-drawn-out scream echoed over the rooftops.

'Listen to that! They're coming to kill us all!' Quilley screamed.

'So what does that mean?' asked Jacob.

'It means that unless you do as I say, you're going to die! Die! Death! Death, get used to the word!' All the bitter years of Quilley's emotional exile poured out of him.

'Well, we all terminate sooner or later,' said someone in the crowd to nods of approval. 'Why get all wrong-feeling about it?'

Quilley was beginning to think he should heed the Doctor's words and abandon them, but a surge of what must have been nobility kept him in place for one last try. 'And do you want to die sooner or later?' he spat.

He caught Lene's eyes as they produced tears for the very first time. 'I'm going to die,' she said in a terrified voice.

'So come with me. Now!' barked Quilley.

He grabbed Lene's hand and dragged her up in the direction of the steps. Jacob followed, though Quilley supposed he didn't quite know why.

The rest of the crowd remained in the street, huddling together uneasily.

The female Hy-Bractor lurched around a corner, teeth wide and glinting redly. 'Hello,' she rasped. 'You must be humans.'

The crowd flinched as one, but nobody ran.

The Hy-Bractor held up a piece of paper and checked the crowd against it. 'And none of you are him with the leather jacket, or Chantal, or one of my friends either, so...'

She shot out an enormously muscled black-suited

arm and picked up the nearest human. The others stood and watched as her massive jaw clicked back on a hinge mechanism, gaping even wider…

And then the crowd screamed, but they remained standing still.

In the lift, Quilley frantically thumbed the button to go up. 'There's no need to keep pressing it. You only need to do it once,' said Jacob, who was cradling the sobbing form of Lene in his arms.

With a clunk, the lift started to ascend. Quilley slumped against the wall and stared at him with contempt.

After catching up on each other's news, Rose had got Tillun to lead the Doctor right back to the tribe, running ahead of her and the Doctor on the horse.

'Was this a wild horse?' Rose had asked.

'It was livid,' said the Doctor.

'And you tamed it? Doesn't that take weeks?'

'Not when you've got this,' said the Doctor, brandishing his slightly psychic paper. 'It thinks I'm wonderful, god of the horses. Does pictures too, you know, psychic paper.'

Back at the cave entrance she introduced the Doctor as an elder of the Tylers, but this didn't seem to count for much.

'I'm the wise woman of this tribe!' Nan shouted in his face. 'Who the blinking hell are you to order us about?'

'Did she really say blinking?' asked Rose.

'That's the TARDIS – got a swear filter,' the Doctor told her. He turned back to face Nan, who viewed him with open suspicion. 'And I'm the wise man of mine!'

Nan scoffed and a ripple of laughter passed round the tribe. 'Wise man! Man! Men in charge, we all know how that ends up!'

'No, you don't, and you never will, unless your people get deep down into the caves!' shouted the Doctor. 'You cannot win against this new tribe, but you could buy me a few hours to get rid of them for you!'

Nan laughed. 'We're the hardest tribe for miles around. No one's gonna try tangling with us.' There was a general nodding of heads. 'And we don't take the word of an outsider. Anyone outside the Family is a liar.'

'Typical blinking human parochialism,' said the Doctor.

Rose stepped forward. 'Hold on. Nan, would you take my word?'

'You turned your back on us, wandering off! You're a nice girl, Rose, but you're still an outsider,' said Nan.

'But I don't have to be,' said Rose. 'You want me to join the Family. If I did, would you listen to me? If I told you something that was for the good of the tribe?'

Nan wrinkled up her face. 'I'd have to.'

'Stone Age psychology,' Rose whispered to the bemused Doctor. Then she grabbed Tillun by the hand. 'OK, let's do it. Quick. Get the Great Fish of Matrimony.'

Nan beamed. 'Now you're being sensible. There's still time…' She turned to the gathered tribe and shouted, 'The wedding's going ahead!'

'Sooner the better,' urged Rose. She turned to the Doctor, daring him to pass a remark. 'Breathe one word of this to my mother or Mickey…'

'Congratulations,' was all the Doctor could say.

ELEVEN

Rose examined the huge smelly trout Nan had handed her. 'Not quite how I ever imagined it,' she told the Doctor.

'That's a good fish,' he said. 'Living right next to a stream with fish like that pouring down it, this lot are affluent for the period. They won't need to do much to keep themselves alive.' He smiled. 'The closest you'll ever get to the Garden of Eden.'

'This is paradise?' Rose sighed, looking on as the tribe gathered in a rough semicircle to watch the ceremony. Tillun had returned to the cave, to be brought out when the sun hit the stone.

'Yeah,' said the Doctor. 'And it also proves that *Carry On Cleo* was more historically accurate than anyone realised.'

Rose shot him a sidelong glance. 'You're very relaxed for someone being chased by monsters.'

'You get used to it,' said the Doctor. He tapped his skull. 'And the brain's operational again. I think I can work out what to do. In a bit.'

'You might say thanks,' said Rose.

The Doctor shrugged. 'Just a bit of paper. And marrying for love, it's overrated.'

'Like you'd know.'

'Who says I don't?' said the Doctor brightly. 'Ask Lady Mary Wortley Montagu.'

Rose decided to let that one pass. 'So, marrying to save a tribe of cavemen from some monsters, that's a good reason, then?'

'You might save the world,' said the Doctor. 'Best reason of all.'

'I'm not sure I wanna join the Family,' said Rose. 'They look all right, but they hate the Neanderthals. They attack them, just for something to do.'

'That's humans. Anyone outside the tribe's some sort of evil animal,' said the Doctor.

'Knew it'd all be our fault,' said Rose.

'Generally is,' said the Doctor.

Rose blinked and ran a hand through her hair. 'So we're not just thick, we're evil? Why d'you hang around us so much, then?'

The Doctor looked into her eyes, serious. 'You can be brilliant, terrible, generous, cruel. But you're never boring.'

A tribesman dressed in a garland of flowers, evidently some kind of officiating priest, ran up to them, slapped Rose with another oily fish and shouted, 'Let the ceremony begin!'

'See,' said the Doctor.

Quilley led Jacob and Lene through the woods, wheezing from the exertion. They were about a mile away now and he let himself slip down onto a fallen tree trunk. His ribs creaked. He put a hand to his forehead and mopped away the sweat. Lene crashed down next to him.

'Why have we stopped?' asked Jacob.

'Not all of us had the health patches,' Quilley growled up at him.

'We have,' said Jacob hesitantly. 'So Lene and I, we could keep on running.'

Quilley put his head in his hands. 'First, Lene is sick. And second, I just saved your lives, so you owe me.' Jacob opened his mouth to speak, but Quilley held up a hand to prevent him. 'If you ask why I shall probably kill you myself.'

Jacob held Lene, whose face was covered in dirt and tears. 'I don't know why I'm running at all,' she said slowly. 'I'm going to terminate… die anyway. I'm so…' She couldn't find the word.

'Afraid,' Quilley finished for her.

'Is this what it was like to Refuse?' she asked.

Quilley nodded. 'More or less.'

Lene choked. 'Then we were right. You must have been insane.'

Tillun strode from the cave entrance to a round of applause from the tribe. Nan and Gual walked slowly behind him. A garland of flowers had been placed on his head and he looked suitably proud and kingly.

The procession came to a halt before the Doctor and Rose. The priest-figure stepped forward, rattled a few bones, and sang, 'Turn to the stone of Brelalla!'

Rose obeyed. At exactly the right moment, the setting sun touched the tip of the stone, casting a long evening shadow that reached out almost to where they stood.

'Now pass the Great Fish of Matrimony,' intoned the priest.

Rose gratefully handed the fish to Tillun, who proceeded to rip off its head.

'Now kiss!' sang the priest.

Rose took a deep breath and turned to Tillun. He leaned over and gave her the snog of her life. Over her shoulder she heard the Doctor sighing.

'What a terrible ordeal for you,' he muttered, with more than a hint of something that was either envy or fatherly protectiveness, she couldn't tell which.

Rose broke the kiss, gathered herself and muttered back, 'Always the bridesmaid.'

The priest waggled more bones. 'You are now one flesh. The Great Fish of Matrimony names you Rose Glathigacymcilliach!'

The Doctor stepped forward urgently. 'Right, is that it?'

Rose took her cue. She turned to Nan. 'Nan, I'm one of the Family. Listen to the Doctor. You've gotta hide, get down into the caves! Move!'

'My granddaughter has spoken!' cried Nan. 'Flee, my people! Flee!'

Rose felt a combination of relief and astonishment as the tribe turned as one and started running for the caves. Only Tillun stood still, holding her hand. 'How mad is that?' she whispered.

'You're one of them now, Rose Glathigacymcilliach,' said the Doctor.

'Think I just might keep my maiden name,' said Rose.

The Doctor patted Tillun on the back and pointed him in the direction of the cave. 'You hurry along too, sonny boy.'

'My wife, the young queen, is coming with me,' Tillun said protectively.

The Doctor shook his head. 'You'll have to wait for the honeymoon.' To Rose he said, 'We've gotta go and warn the Neanderthals.'

Rose frowned. 'Bigamy is not on today's agenda.'

'Why warn Them?' asked Tillun. 'Perhaps the new tribe will attack Them first. That will give us more time to hide ourselves.'

'I don't suppose you've invented divorce?' said Rose.

The Doctor whistled for his horse, which had been munching happily on a patch of long grass. It cantered up. Tillun stood in front of the Doctor. 'Rose comes with us. She isn't one of the Tylers any longer!'

'Sorry, haven't got time to argue,' said the Doctor, lifting Rose up onto the horse.

Tillun was astonished. He launched himself at the Doctor, hands reaching for his neck.

The Doctor parried the attack with ease, tripping Tillun onto the hard ground and then leaning over to whisper in his ear, 'It's a nasty feeling, being used. Sorry. But don't worry. There's plenty more, er, fish in the sea.'

With that, he leaped onto the horse and effortlessly turned it in the right direction. 'Let's head to the forest. Know the way?'

'I had a bag over my head,' said Rose. 'No idea.'

'We'll find 'em,' said the Doctor, prodding the horse gently with his foot.

It tore off, giving Rose a jolt so hard she was forced to wrap her arms around the Doctor's middle. She gave a last glance at Tillun, who was picking himself up, a look of hurt and confusion on his face.

'You enjoyed that,' Rose told the Doctor accusingly.

The Doctor said nothing, and Rose wished she could see the expression on his face.

'So, how are we gonna stop these Hy-Bractors?' she asked.

'Working it out,' said the Doctor brightly.

The Doctor and Rose left the horse at the edge of the forest. The smell of woodsmoke from the Neanderthals' fire took the Doctor unerringly along one of the trampled-down paths that led to the encampment. Rose's bare flesh was constantly scratched by the brambles and nettles that grew everywhere but she barely paid the discomfort any attention. She was desperate to get to the Neanderthals and save them, to repay a little of the kindness they had shown to her.

'It was a Hy-Bractor that nearly attacked us before, then?' she asked.

'Yeah,' said the Doctor, forcing his way through an especially rough patch of vegetation. 'Chantal let one of them out the back for a roam, to get it trained up. That's our only advantage. They're like children, their brains haven't properly formed yet. There's so much for them to take in.'

'But what are they?' Rose persisted. 'And why's Chantal doing this? What made her wake up one morning and say, "I know, I'll go back in time and breed some rampaging zombies to kill everyone in the Stone Age"?'

The Doctor's reply never came. Instead, seeing something up ahead, framed by the fading twilight, he exhaled a long sigh of relief. 'Yes! Made it in time. The Hy-Bractors must still be down in Osterberg. Fantastic!'

Rose pushed past him. And there was the Neanderthal camp, much as it had been when she last saw it. But the raid by the humans seemed to have left only four of them alive. They were sitting cross-legged, staring into the fire. Rose was relieved to see Sakka and her child among them.

'Doctor, there were about fifty of them,' she said, overcome by the horror of it all. 'And my new family slaughtered them.'

The Doctor looked across at her sadly. 'That's the way it is here,' he said uncomfortably. 'Neanderthals are better fighters than humans – at least in the forest. If we warn them they might stand a better chance, but that's all we can do.'

She couldn't take that. 'I get it. Different morality, get used to it. But I don't want to. It's sick, inhuman.'

'No,' said the Doctor. 'Inhuman, Rose – that's you. Because you care, because you believe in something better. You've seen the future. Humanity is gonna achieve so much, Rose, out in the stars – in spite of itself.' He smiled. 'Look, we've swapped sides.'

'And what about them?' Rose indicated the small, sad group in the clearing. 'They die, and it's history, and no one cares. Just a little bit of genocide along the way to building a mighty space empire? And that's just "the way it is here"?'

The Doctor took her hand. 'If I'm right, the Hy-Bractors could breed, spread out, eventually kill everyone on this planet. We can stop *that* genocide. We must.'

Rose tried to push her feelings to the back of her mind and ran out into the clearing. 'Sakka!' she called. 'Sakka, there are creatures coming and they're worse than anything you've seen before. You've gotta get ready and go!'

Sakka looked up at her dully. The other Neanderthals kept their heads down. She found it hard to imagine the grief they must be going through.

'Rose,' said the Doctor from behind her, very quietly.

'You could give me a hand!' she called back.

Then she turned to see him standing next to something that looked like a weird kind of sculpture, set to one side of the clearing. It was difficult to make it out distinctly in the fading light, but it was of roughly pyramidal shape. It didn't look like anything the Neanderthals could have made. She stepped closer.

It was a huge pyramid of bones. Heavy Neanderthal skulls, ribcages, legs, arms, pelvic bones, arranged neatly, almost artistically.

'Humans didn't do this,' said the Doctor quietly. 'The flesh has been eaten away, every last morsel picked off. The Hy-Bractors have been here. These are their leftovers. They're tidy eaters.'

A wave of pure terror washed over Rose. She looked back at Sakka and the other survivors. 'How did they escape?'

'They were left here as bait,' said a familiar chatty voice. 'Which worked, I'm happy to say.'

The Doctor and Rose whirled round. Chantal had entered the clearing from the other side, the four Hy-Bractors ranged obediently around her.

Rose couldn't restrain herself. She made to launch herself at Chantal, but the Doctor held her back. 'It's pointless.'

Chantal walked forward. 'I need you, Doctor, but Rose – she's just another human. Wasteful, aggressive, untidy…'

The Doctor bit his lip. 'Harm one hair of her head and I'll destroy you.'

Chantal smiled. 'Exactly the reaction I expected. I'm not going to underestimate you again, Doctor. The drugs obviously don't work, so I'm going to ask you to come quietly or I shall let the Hy-Bractors do what comes naturally and tear her limb from limb. She'll make a nice, smooth dessert course after all this hairy lot. I'm worried the Hy-Bractors will start coughing up furballs…'

The Doctor fixed Chantal with a penetrating stare. 'I warn you. Stop this now or I will stop it.'

There was no reaction. Her glassy stare met his unflinchingly, casually.

'That will only work on a person with what you'd call a conscience,' Chantal continued. 'And I patched mine out years ago. Let's go, shall we?'

As the Hy-Bractors lurched into life, coming towards them, the Doctor shouted, 'Run!'

Rose obeyed, but she hadn't gone more than a few paces before she was knocked to the ground. At first she thought something had struck her, but as she writhed in the muddy grass she saw Chantal holding one of the stinger sound weapons. The noise was so loud it drilled into her skull. In the moment before she blacked out she saw the Doctor falling to his knees. They were both the prisoners of this murderous madwoman.

TWELVE

The first thing the Doctor saw when he awoke was the TARDIS standing in all its reassuringly blue, four-square glory. The second thing he saw were the loops of coiled wire strapping him to the chair back in the examination room.

Chantal stepped in front of the TARDIS. 'Pretty easy job for the Hy-Bractors, finding that. Might I suggest you disguise it?'

'It is disguised,' said the Doctor, rather wounded. He nodded to his bonds. 'Oh, look, I'm tied up. Shouldn't have shown you that idea.'

Chantal stroked his forehead gently. 'Come on, Doctor, if you're so clever you must have figured me out by now.'

'You're not like the others here. Much more intelligent.'

'My mother was a pharma-tech,' said Chantal. 'On my seventeenth birthday she implanted an experimental patch designed to increase intelligence exponentially.'

'Makes a change from driving lessons,' said the Doctor.

'My intelligence raced ahead. I learned everything

there was to know. I designed new patches and worked on hundreds of different bio-projects. I patched out my empathy with other humans – it kept getting in the way.' She paused. 'Then I designed the Hy-Bractor. An upgrade of the human race.'

'You call that an upgrade?' scoffed the Doctor. 'Why didn't you call them Human version 2.0?'

'The ones you've seen are just the first,' said Chantal. 'When fully grown, they will be infinitely more adaptable, intelligent and creative than humans, and will lack the basic design flaws.'

'Flaws like what?' asked the Doctor.

Chantal stared into space. 'We'd mapped out the body and the brain to take away all the wrong-feeling. We were an utterly serene and peaceful people. But I knew it couldn't last. I examined the historical record – sooner or later, for whatever reason, the basic human was going to reassert itself. There would be war, horror and misery. My compassionate values couldn't let that happen.'

'I'm just gonna ignore that last sentence,' said the Doctor.

'There is a self-destructive drive in humankind,' Chantal went on. 'Homo sapiens adapted as hunters in a cold environment. But in just a few centuries' time, the climate will change again. Humans will thrive in the warm. They will very quickly abandon the life of the hunter, for which they are adapted, and become farmers.'

'This is turning into *Horizon*,' said a familiar voice away to the Doctor's left.

His neck was restrained so he couldn't turn to see her, but he called out casually, 'Hiya, Rose.'

'Wotcher,' came Rose's reply.

'Complex urban societies will form,' continued Chantal. 'Every human generation building on the achievements of the last – fast-paced cultural evolution. There will be social stratification, class and caste distinctions, violence and inequality. Because the violent, competitive hunting brain of the human will remain. Humans can adapt their environment, but they cannot adapt themselves.'

'Thought your lot had,' said Rose.

'They only suppressed it,' said the Doctor. 'Handed themselves over to the drugs.' He addressed Chantal. 'What you wanted to do was make the change permanent. Build a better species.'

Chantal nodded primly. She still spoke calmly and evenly, in her piping secretary's voice. 'Yes. Ruthless in its dispatch of inferior human competitors. And cooperative, diverse, with stronger values.'

'Values?' spluttered Rose's voice. 'Like slaughtering a village full of Neanderthals without one glance back?'

'Excuse me, Rose, whose species is going to do that anyway?' said Chantal, giggling. 'I don't need a lecture on that from a human.'

'And I don't need a lecture from you but I'm getting one,' replied Rose.

'You must have loved it when you heard the time project was gonna happen,' the Doctor told Chantal.

'I installed myself as director,' said Chantal. 'It was

very easy. I found out who else was being interviewed for the post and I killed them.'

'What is this, the psychopath's guide to career building?' said Rose.

'Plus I had an excellently prepared CV,' continued Chantal. 'The humans of my time are easy prey. They don't run, even when you're pulling them to bits. And all you have to do is give their friends and associates combo 199/87 and they forget they even existed and go happily on their way.'

The Doctor believed he could see it now. 'So the idea was to come back here and breed your Hy-Bractors?'

Chantal nodded. 'I disabled the time engine, cutting off contact with the other end. Then I diverted the power to the area behind the Grey Door, where the Hy-Bractors were cultivated. It took forty-eight days to fully gestate four of them, and there will be many more.'

'So,' said the Doctor, 'you'll let them swarm over the planet, breed, kill all their competitors, Neanderthal and human alike – tape over centuries of history with your own barmy Utopia.'

'To create the world humans always wanted but could never achieve,' said Chantal, her voice still even and expressionless. 'No wish unfulfilled, no love to turn away, no life wasted. But with their bestial, unadapted hunting minds they could never have it, never triumph against themselves.' Her voice rose. 'The Hy-Bractors will not have that problem! They are adapted perfectly for Earth!'

There was a silence. 'Well, whoopee for the Hy-

Bractors,' said the Doctor eventually.

'OK, how are we gonna stop her?' Rose called over.

'Working it out,' he replied.

Chantal studied the Doctor closely. 'I'm fascinated, Doctor. Why do you *want* to stop me?'

Rose cut in before the Doctor could answer. 'One, you're a total fruitloop. Two, you've killed loads of people. Three, you've got a really annoying whingeing voice –'

'I asked him, thanks, Rose,' interrupted Chantal. 'What I have done is good,' she told the Doctor.

'Four, the ends never justify the means,' added Rose.

'Please shut it,' said Chantal warningly.

The Doctor beamed up at her. 'Rose is dead right. All those reasons, but especially two and four.'

'Thanks,' Rose called.

'Any time,' the Doctor called back. He wished he could turn round and see her, check that she was all right. 'Oh, and five,' he told Chantal, 'you want the TARDIS, to spread your upgrade all through space and time. Am I right or what?'

'Correct,' said Chantal.

'That's not going to happen,' said the Doctor.

Chantal gave him a strange smile. 'Is it not?'

The Doctor was taken aback. It was hard to threaten somebody who didn't possess a full personality. The Doctor had learned over centuries of travel how to scare bad people, to stare them in the eye and make them squirm. But, as with the other Osterbergers, there was nothing to latch on to behind Chantal's eyes.

Rose's voice cut across his train of thought. 'Doctor,

when I just said all that, I wanted to count it out on my fingers, yeah? But they feel weird.'

'She's got you strapped down, same as me,' the Doctor called.

'No, I can feel them,' said Rose. 'But it's like they're… miles away.'

The Doctor struggled in his bonds. He shouted to Chantal, 'What have you done to her?'

'She's an available resource,' said Chantal clinically.

Somehow, thought the Doctor, it would have been easier if she'd said it with lip-smacking relish, but it came out in the same dry way. 'Personal emotional attachments are one of the major flaws of the human, essential for the bonding of small hunting communities but not needed in more advanced and successful urban environments.'

The Doctor wrestled frantically in his bonds.

Chantal looked down. 'They're obviously a flaw in your species too. That's interesting.'

'What have you done to her?' the Doctor repeated.

'This,' said Chantal. She went behind the Doctor's chair and swung it round.

On a table at the other end of the room was Rose's head. Her face was as animated as ever.

Chantal leaned over the Doctor and whispered in his ear, 'If you want her put back together –' she pointed to the TARDIS – 'then you will give me what I want.'

THIRTEEN

'Rose,' said the Doctor calmly. 'Don't look down.'

'I can't look down,' said Rose. 'I can't move my head.'

'Good,' said the Doctor.

'What's good about it?' Rose demanded. 'What's she done to me?'

The Doctor licked his lips. 'Nothing I can't fix.'

'Nothing *I* can't fix,' Chantal corrected. 'Now…' She indicated the TARDIS again.

'I'm gonna have to stand up,' the Doctor pointed out.

Chantal took the cutter from her trolley of instruments and sliced through the restraining loops. 'Please do. But remember – only I can put things back the way they were. So any kind of opposition to me would be a very, very bad idea, wouldn't it?'

The Doctor got up from the chair and walked slowly over to the TARDIS. 'This is the TARDIS, then. Time And Relative Dimension In Space. Can go anywhere in –'

'Blah-de-blah, heard all that,' said Chantal. 'Open it up.'

The Doctor felt in his pocket for the key. It wasn't

there. He put out his hand and Chantal produced it from her suit, dropping it in his hand.

'Wouldn't open for you, then?' said the Doctor.

'But I'm sure it'll open for you,' said Chantal.

Rose looked on with alarm as the Doctor raised the key to the lock of the TARDIS. She didn't understand the strange way she felt, as if her body was somehow separated from her, but her worries about that were superseded by the prospect of a nutter like Chantal getting into the TARDIS.

'Doctor, what are you doing!' she called out, and tried to take a step forward. As she did, there was a rattling noise from a metal cabinet at the other end of the room.

The Doctor looked at the cabinet, then over at Rose. 'Did you just try and step forward?'

Rose was confused. 'Yeah. I thought I did... It's weird. It's like there's a door or something in my way, but there can't be...'

'Safely tucked away for later,' Chantal told the Doctor with a significant look to the cabinet. She indicated the door of the TARDIS. 'Now, open it.'

The Doctor paused for a moment and then held the key up in front of Chantal's face. 'Right, well, this key works on a kind of meson projection recognition system...' He cut himself off. 'Look, it's gonna be very hard explaining all this to someone like you. Backward, evil and brainy-thick, that's quite a tough one.'

'Evil,' tutted Chantal. 'Morality exists only as an evolutionary safeguard in primitive conscious species.

It has no physical existence or meaning outside their minds.'

'Ever heard the phrase *reductio ad absurdum*?' asked the Doctor. 'No, probably not. It's all chemicals and genes and design to you.'

Rose realised that the Doctor was trying to distract Chantal. It was a method she'd used on teachers at school to pass the time. Get them talking about something they were obsessed by, unions or cheese or whatever, and take their mind off the class. The Doctor was buying time for her – but she had no idea what she was supposed to do. She flexed her fingers, trying to work out if she'd been drugged numb from the neck down or something. Her fingers moved the way they always did, but it was as if they weren't connected to her, as if they belonged to somebody else. It was an unpleasant, powerless sensation and she couldn't see how she could help the Doctor. She put out her hand and touched something. It felt like a doorknob. She gave it a rattle –

and heard that rattle coming from the other end of the room.

'Like,' the Doctor continued in a loud voice, addressing Chantal, 'if you were designing a door handle – easiest, most practical thing in the universe, all you have to do is reach out, twist and pull – no, you'd have to add some kind of smarty-boots spin, redesign the human hand with three thumbs or something.' He emphasised the words *door*, *handle* and *hand*.

Rose understood – he wanted her to open the door. She could feel it, and hear it, but if she was over here and the cabinet was over there, how?

An earlier remark of the Doctor's swam back to her. *These people are experts with the body. They can do anything to it. They could probably take you apart and put you together again.*

A nauseous feeling turned her distant stomach over. It couldn't be... She nearly fainted, but the Doctor's insistent voice pulled her back to the instant. He was relying on her. So what if her head was no longer attached to her body?

'Still got pride, I notice,' he was saying to Chantal. 'You've booted that right up.'

'That's an essential. Pride in the superiority of the Hy-Bractor,' said Chantal. 'Anyway, stop trying to delay me. Let's get back to your door, which you are about to open.'

'OK,' said the Doctor. 'Yeah, unlike other simple, convenient doors like the people here would make and anyone could open, this is a complex refracting multi-tumbler –'

Rose took a deep breath, which she distinctly felt entering her mouth over here and filling her lungs over there – how that worked she couldn't figure out. Then she grabbed the handle and stepped out of the cabinet. She saw her headless body, still dressed in the skin wedding outfit, step out on the other side of the room and couldn't hold herself back from exclaiming, 'Oh, my God!'

Chantal turned, and in the second she was distracted, the Doctor grabbed the cutter from her and held her, struggling, in an armlock. 'It's gonna be OK, Rose!' he shouted.

Rose said the first thing that came into her head. 'My arms are quite long, aren't they?'

'You forgot something,' the Doctor told Chantal, manhandling her back over to the chair. 'Some humans are really smart.'

'Do you mean me?' asked Rose, still captivated by her body. She tried walking around a bit, but it was difficult, a bit like pushing a shopping trolley one way only to find it goes the other. Her left and right were mixed up.

The Doctor leaned over Chantal. 'Rose didn't just freak. Why? Cos she trusts me. Why? Cos she likes me. Why? Cos, boiling it all back down to your precious drawing board, she's designed to like people who like her. Thank you, blind chaotic nature, big up to you!'

'But unfortunately for you, I'm smarter,' said Chantal.

With a sudden, savage movement she pulled another cutter from her pocket and swung it at the Doctor. He tried to parry the blow, but with ferocious strength she kicked him to the floor. Winded, the Doctor took a moment to get to his feet. When he did, he saw Rose's body flailing at Chantal, the cutter whizzing about between them.

'Nutter!' shouted Rose.

'I don't care what you think,' said Chantal.

'Makes me feel better saying it,' said Rose.

The Doctor looked around. On the trolley were an array of instruments and a couple of popper packs. He grabbed both of the packs and dialled a combination of numbers on each, then, as Rose's body kicked

Chantal away from itself, he stepped forward and pushed them onto either side of her chest.

For a second Chantal's mouth formed an 'O' of surprise. Then she dropped the cutter and smiled. 'Thanks,' she said.

'A dose of combo 199/87,' said the Doctor, looking rather pleased with himself. He guided Chantal to the chair and sat her down. 'Now we could do anything to her. Tear her to bits and she wouldn't care.'

'I'm all for a bit of poetic justice,' said Rose. 'But I'm the one who's in bits.' She walked her body over to her head and examined it. 'I've got a pretty good tummy button.'

'Don't worry. We'll sort that out later,' he said confidently. 'Still got to work the main thing out. The Hy-Bractors roaming around up there.'

Rose's body kicked him. 'I can't spend the rest of my life like this!'

'I'll fix you up, don't worry,' said the Doctor, not very reassuringly. He started ransacking the cupboards and cabinets. 'The Hy-Bractors are superior to humans by design, right? Better design, humans don't stand a chance against them, they're just prey. Unless humans had…' He found a piece of equipment in a corner – a long metal box with a keyboard set into the top – and jumped for joy. 'That's it! Fantastic! Worked it out!'

He set to work frantically, dialling codes into the machine so quickly that his fingers seemed to blur.

Quilley, Jacob and Lene sat still in the pitch blackness of their forest hideout. They could hear a Hy-Bractor, seemingly just a few feet away from them, trampling through the greenery and cooing gently to keep itself company.

'Looking for humans,' it mumbled. 'Kill all the humans…'

Lene whimpered. Quilley couldn't think of anything to do. He remembered reading about hopeless situations like this in the old books, and how he and Elaina had laughed at the illogical way the characters sometimes responded when all hope was lost. Now he understood why they did what they did.

He took the hands of Jacob and Lene and mouthed the illogical words silently: 'Our Father, which art in heaven…'

'Yeah, but what are you doing?' Rose demanded.

The Doctor had produced a phial of serum from the machine and was now riffling desperately through the rest of the stores. 'Fighting fire with fire.'

'Can I help or shall I just stand about?' asked Rose.

'Yeah, hold that,' he said, handing her body the serum. He delved deep into the storage cabinet where her body had been hidden away and picked out something that looked like a cross between a nozzle deodorant spray and a machine gun. 'Yes! I knew she had to have something like this!' He took the serum back from Rose and slotted it into a cavity at the rear of the device. 'I can see why evolution normally takes millions of years. And I've got only minutes.'

'You've evolved something?'

'Not really. Adapted a gene, just like Chantal did

when she bred the Hy-Bractors, and force-cultivated it so it's incredibly potent. Added it to some lactobacilli she had hanging about.'

Rose knew the word from commercials. 'The stuff you get in yoghurt?'

The Doctor nodded. 'Bacteria of the gut. Friendly little parasite. I can use it to spread my mixture.' He tapped the serum and cocked the device on his shoulder like a gun.

'And what's in your mixture?'

'An advantage,' said the Doctor. 'A gift for the humans and the Neanderthals.' Then he raced towards the door. 'Back in a bit. If not, get into the TARDIS and let it take you to Bromley again.'

As he dashed out Rose sighed and sat her body down on the floor. 'Where I'm gonna fit right in,' she said ruefully.

Tillun had not returned to the cave with the others. He struck out after his wife on foot, heading for the Neanderthal camp, spear at his side. He smarted from the snub and was deeply suspicious of the Doctor. That story about the dangerous new tribe seemed to him just a good excuse to get everyone distracted while he took Rose away. But Rose was his queen now and, for the honour of the tribe, she must be retrieved. To travel alone at night was foolhardy, but it would be better to die than be made a fool of by the big-nosed stranger. Tillun's heart burned with righteous anger spawned by his humiliation.

Then, suddenly, he heard something moving in the

forest up ahead. He flung himself flat on the ground.

The moonlight picked out a huge shape – like a man, but not a man. It walked with terrifying complacency through this dangerous place, as if nothing could challenge it. That nonchalance was the most frightening thing about it, though Tillun swallowed convulsively in terror at its long, whipping tail and gross, lumpy features.

'Human!' it cried.

Somehow, it had seen him.

He broke from cover. He knew he could not fight this huge, powerfully muscular beast, so he turned to run. But in three quick strides the beast caught up with him and lifted him off his feet. It dangled him in the air, swinging him about to face it.

'No, you're not him in the jacket, or Chantal,' it said slowly, 'or one of my friends, so...'

The Doctor ran through the streets of Osterberg. They were lined with skeletons, arranged in neat pyramidal piles. It was a city of the dead, and unless his plan worked, he had no doubt the entire planet would eventually follow suit as the Hy-Bractors bred and fed. He tested the device, spraying invisible particles into the air.

As he dived through the lift doors and thumbed the button to ascend, he heard a familiar voice call, 'Stop! You in the jacket!'

He looked back. The first Hy-Bractor, X01, was at the foot of the steps.

The doors closed and the lift started to go up.

The Doctor shuddered. Rose was still down there – and the Hy-Bractor was down there with her. He shouldered the spray device and patted it. This had to work. His calculations had to be correct. Or Rose would die with the rest of them.

Chantal, lying back on the chair and staring wide-eyed at the ceiling, was singing lightly to herself. It was starting to irritate Rose. She walked herself over to her head, picked it up and carried it back to Chantal to frown down at her.

'Put a sock in it,' she told her.

'Hello, Rose,' said Chantal dreamily. 'How are you?'

'Don't know what you're so happy about,' said Rose. 'We've beaten you.'

Chantal shrugged. 'Really? Who cares?' She started singing again.

The door of the examination room was thrust open. Rose turned, expecting to see the Doctor. 'That was quick –'

'Human!' said the Hy-Bractor as it lurched in.

'I think it's going to kill you, Rose,' said Chantal.

The Doctor burst out from the lift into the bitingly cold night air. He hefted the spray device, pulled the trigger and turned a full circle.

'Now! Do your stuff! Work your magic! Go!'

'Don't think I'll stay to watch. It might give me a wrong-feeling,' said Chantal as the Hy-Bractor advanced on Rose.

Rose was dimly aware of Chantal slipping out of the examination room. She backed away from the Hy-Bractor, tucking her head under her arm.

What a way to go.

The female Hy-Bractor parted the bracken that concealed Quilley, Jacob and Lene.

Quilley closed his eyes and prepared for death. He didn't feel gallant or noble any longer. There was just a dull, aching sensation tugging at his heart. For the first time in many years he wished he had a popper pack.

And then, suddenly, he felt different. He looked at the Hy-Bractor and wanted to laugh. What kind of a threat was that?

He didn't know why he was feeling this way.

The Hy-Bractor lunged for him.

And as if it was the most natural, ordinary thing in the world, T. P. Quilley opened his mouth wide and blew its head off with a sheet of flaming acid.

The Hy-Bractor's body toppled backwards with a shattering crash.

Quilley stood up and swallowed hard. The flame went out.

'I'm quite sure I've never done that before,' he said.

A ball of liquid fire shot from Tillun's mouth and the Hy-Bractor slumped headless to the ground.

'I must be a god,' said Tillun, trying to make sense of what had just happened.

The Hy-Bractor towered over Rose.

Before she could even really think about it, as casually as she might swat an irritating fly, she held up her head and spat fire.

Jack will be leaving tomorrow. The Doctor and Rose are returning, and he must resume his life as a traveller. I think he must be insane. No other world could be better than this one.

Of course I often think of my old life, but less and less. It's hard to miss it – especially now I have my job and Anna Marie and crisps. Here everybody is very different. In my old world we all did the same things and spoke many of the same thoughts.

Anna Marie is very beautiful. She came round to the flat and we kissed, ate crisps and chocolate, and watched television. Her favourite television tribe is a real one, of famous people who have achieved much. They have been exiled to an island to see if they will fall in love. Anna Marie reads the special shining books called magazines that tell her what all the famous people are doing. She makes a special drink called a spritzer which we like. She thinks I am from Romania and doesn't ask me many questions about it, so I don't have to make up too many lies.

I think Jack is jealous of me. He gives Anna Marie very odd looks and shakes his head, and they don't get along very well. She uses unfriendly words to describe him and says he dresses just a bit too young.

I'm enjoying my job. We are making some new flats from bricks and mortar. It's very simple and I enjoy lifting things. The men I work with are good friends and we laugh a lot together. Often we all lie to our boss about how much work we have done.

Jack has bought me many books to read, but I prefer the magazines. I won't be too sad when Jack goes. I'm grateful to him for looking after me, but I think now I belong here more than he does. I enjoy the boredom and all the eating, thinking and learning, but Jack likes things to happen and more tension in general, and wants to get back to the TARDIS. He enjoys danger and fighting, which, if you ask me, is stupid.

Yesterday I decided to ask Anna Marie to become my mate, which is called marrying here. She said yes right away, and we will have our wedding soon. She took me to meet her mother and father. Her mother is another fine, fat woman. Her father took me to one side and cried. He said he had always been worried that Anna Marie would never meet a nice man and that he was very happy I had come along. I didn't understand at first, as Anna Marie's sister is hideous – thin as a stick – and she is already married. But then I remembered that the humans think smoothness is sexy.

I must stop thinking of myself as different. Soon I will have a wife and we will live together. Anna

Marie would like to have children. Jack says this will be possible. I would like Anna Marie to have a good number of children, say about three. I will name them after the people who helped me. They will be called Jack, Rose and the Doctor.

Captain Jack Harkness's Data-Record

Time's almost up. And my work here is done.

Das has got himself a fiancée. I'd say she has more trouble fitting in than he does, which is kind of cute. And to him, yeah, she's a real calendar girl. A face only a mother or a Neanderthal could love.

My heels are itching. I've never been confined to one planet this long – at least not without some plan hatching – and I worry it's starting to contaminate me. I saw a poster in a travel agent's window this morning and caught myself thinking Australia looked interesting. Very bad sign.

Peacetime is a bit freaky. Everyone here – including Das – has that deadly combination of contentment and ennui. Without the flavour of danger, without the constant lurking threat of death, life's one long, slow afternoon watching VH1 Smooth. When they talk about how stressed they are you've gotta laugh. Yeah, your trains don't run on time, big deal. Try living in a city under siege by the Varionette Ministerium, that's stress.

It's kind of hard to believe Rose comes from here

– she's so much more alive. I guess that's why the Doctor picked her.

I miss those two. When the TARDIS pops up tomorrow it's gonna be all I can do not to run in and give them both a smacker on the lips. Life with the Doctor and Rose is the best you're gonna get.

Next stop – Kegron Pluva, please, and cross fingers there'll be a war on.

Fourteen

Things had gone wrong, Chantal realised. Her plans had come to nothing, thwarted by the Doctor.

Hey-ho, she thought. Never mind. Life goes on. Start again.

She sauntered through the streets of Osterberg, round the tidy piles of human bones, trying to come up with a new scheme. She was sure the drugs pumping through her body were not quite enough to fully knock out her intelligence patch. There'd be an idea along soon enough.

It arrived, and she laughed and smote her forehead. Well, *obviously*…

She made her way to the time engine and her hands ran absently over the levers and wheels that controlled it, switching the power outlet from the Grey Door back to the engine itself. The machine chugged away furiously, steam blowing out of either end, and a beam of green light formed. Chantal was looking forward to her new life in the twenty-first century. She would deliver value. Get herself a nice job, something scientific, and then eradicate the poor, sad human race just as she'd intended. This was only a mini-setback.

*

The Doctor raced into the examination room to be greeted with an extraordinary sight. A Hy-Bractor lay dead on the floor, only a scorched stump left where its head had been. Rose was lifting her own head up to peer down at it.

'I did it!' said the Doctor, punching the air. 'I worked it out and I did it!'

'Are all the Hy-Bractors dead?' asked Rose.

'If they're not, they soon will be,' replied the Doctor. 'Can't bring myself to feel gutted. Where's Chantal?' He looked about.

'Doctor.' Rose held out her head and spat another ball of flame that went over his shoulder.

'Don't worry, it's only a temporary adaptation,' said the Doctor airily. 'It'll last just long enough for the people here to survive. Fade in a while. Where's Chantal?'

'Doctor!' Rose held up her head again meaningfully, gesturing at her body with her eyes.

'Oh yeah,' said the Doctor. 'Where's Chantal? She can sort that out.'

Rose blinked. 'You mean – you *can't*?'

But the Doctor was already out of the door. Taking a deep breath – somehow – Rose and her body followed.

Tillun ran through the forest, exhilarated, stopping every few seconds to test his new, god-given power to spit fire. He could conquer everything! Nan and the others would be proud as he led the tribe to greater and greater glory!

He heard sounds of movement up ahead and

stopped instinctively. Then he remembered that he need fear nothing – not even being alone at night – and ran on, raising his spear and chanting.

Three people were picked out in the moonlit glow. He would challenge them and, if they moved to injure him, he would simply blow them away!

The shortest of the three, who wore a strange head-covering, turned at his approach and blew fire at him before he could come close.

'Oh,' said Tillun, crushed. 'So everyone can do it.'

Quilley edged up to him slowly and put out his hand. 'Good evening, young man.'

'Hello,' said Tillun, sighing.

'She's using the time engine,' said Rose as she followed the Doctor into the steam-filled room. A green glow suffused one corner of the shack, growing in intensity. 'Can't be that bright, can she?'

The Doctor nodded. He shielded his eyes and saw the outline of Chantal through the steam. 'Chantal, listen to me. Don't walk into that beam!'

'Can you give me a good reason why not?' came the cheery reply. 'I don't think so!'

'It'll rip you apart!' shouted the Doctor.

'Not listening,' said Chantal, still in her singsong voice. 'You're trying to put me off, Doctor. I'm too clever for that!'

'More than one trip and your cells get corrupted,' he called out.

'Plus you've gotta put my head back on!' shouted Rose.

'You'll get used to it, love!' Chantal giggled and stepped into the green light.

She had one second longer to exult in her own brightness and charm before every cell in her body reversed and she was torn apart by the time winds.

'Oh, great,' said Rose's head. 'What am I gonna do now? Move to Legoland?'

The Doctor looked worried. 'Could be the least of your problems. Remember what Jack said about rip engines?'

'They blow up,' said Rose.

'And this one's just about to,' said the Doctor. 'Good job too. Don't want any archaeologists digging this place up. Make a brilliant episode of Time Team, but... Back to the TARDIS, quick!' He raced out.

Rose's arm grabbed him and shook her head at him. 'But if there's no more Chantal, who's gonna stick this back on?'

'This whole town is about to explode,' said the Doctor evasively.

The engine roared.

They reached the examination room with seconds to spare. The Doctor grabbed the tray of instruments and drugs from the trolley and swept Rose into the TARDIS.

Rose slammed the door shut and followed him up the ramp. He had switched on the monitor and they watched together as the room outside whited out in a tremendous flash. The ground under the TARDIS wobbled. Rose clung onto her head with one hand

and the console with the other.

'You can do it, can't you?' Rose asked in the silence that followed.

'Of course I can,' said the Doctor. He held up one of Chantal's instruments and clicked it on. 'Well, I can learn.'

Rose licked her lips. 'OK. Joking or not joking?'

'Not joking,' said the Doctor.

The boom of the explosion knocked Quilley, Tillun, Jacob and Lene to the ground.

A moment later Quilley started as an extraordinary groaning noise echoed around them. A blue box with a flashing light on top began to fade up before him. 'Oh dear,' he sighed. 'All my life I wanted emotions. Now I could do with some blankness.'

Tillun stood up and put an arm round him. 'Don't fear,' he said. 'Our fire-mouths can destroy anything!'

The door of the box began to open. Tillun strode up and swallowed, readying himself…

The Doctor's head poked out. Tillun spat – and a gob of saliva landed on the Doctor's nose. 'Thanks, mate,' said the Doctor, rubbing at it. 'Good job I put a time limit on that.'

'Where is my wife?' demanded Tillun. He raised his spear. 'I want her back!'

The Doctor stepped out of the TARDIS, carrying Rose's head under his arm.

'Hiya,' said Rose's head tentatively.

Tillun stared at her, stared at the Doctor, then dropped his spear and ran off backwards into the woods, screaming.

'Must have been something you said,' said the Doctor.

Rose's body emerged from the TARDIS. 'Shame. I could have married worse people.'

'You still might, with your record at picking them,' the Doctor said, before turning to address Quilley, Jacob and Lene. He held up Rose's head. 'Chantal's dust, the Hy-Bractors are all dead –'

Quilley was formulating a reply when the bushes parted and a Hy-Bractor emerged into the clearing.

'Rose, do your stuff!' shouted the Doctor.

'Time limit,' said Rose. 'I don't think gobbing at it's gonna do much good.'

The Hy-Bractor looked around the small group, then pointed to the Doctor. 'You're him, aren't you? Him with the leather jacket?' It waved a piece of paper in his direction with a drawing of the Doctor on it.

'That's me,' said the Doctor slowly. 'Not bad. She captured the ears all right.'

'We aren't supposed to kill you,' said the Hy-Bractor. 'But I can kill all these others...' It started to reach for Quilley.

'No!' shouted the Doctor. He positioned himself in front of the Hy-Bractor. 'You get your orders from Chantal, right?'

'That is correct,' said the Hy-Bractor.

'I'm afraid she's dead,' said the Doctor.

'Oh. So I can eat you now?' said the Hy-Bractor.

'No, no, it doesn't work like that,' said the Doctor hurriedly. He grabbed the piece of paper and drew something on the back. 'You see, before Chantal died, she told me to tell you to only ever eat things that *don't* look like this.'

He turned the paper round to show a rudimentary sketch of a human.

'I see,' said the Hy-Bractor. 'Anything not human.'

'And not to eat too many,' added the Doctor.

The Hy-Bractor took the drawing. 'I shall do that if it's what Chantal wanted.' He lurched off into the undergrowth.

'That was very easy,' said Quilley. 'Will it really follow your instructions?'

'Why not?' said the Doctor brightly. 'It was designed to be better than a human, remember.'

'It can't lie,' said Rose. 'So it can't understand being lied to.'

'So that's about it,' said the Doctor. 'But can you guess what our last problem is?' He raised Rose's head significantly.

Jacob got to his feet. 'Do you want it putting back?'

'No, I love it.' Rose gave him a sarcastic look, forgetting he was an Osterberger and it would be wasted. But to her surprise he returned it with an ironic smile.

The Doctor handed Jacob the instruments. 'Please.'

'I don't know how,' said Jacob.

The Doctor swallowed. He didn't dare look into Rose's eyes, so he kept her head facing away from him.

'I can do it,' said another voice.

Lene was trying to stand up. 'It's easy,' she said weakly. 'All you have to do is reverse-lock the kinetic seal. I used to do it all the time.'

Jacob looked at her anxiously. 'You're too sick. It's a delicate operation.'

Lene took his hand. 'You can help me. That's what a husband is for.' She gave him a smile that was entirely genuine.

Jacob felt a prickling behind his eyes and, though it was a wrong-feeling, wondered how he could ever have lived without it.

The Doctor passed Rose's head to Lene.

Lene settled Rose's head on her shoulders, adjusted it slightly and switched on a tiny spherical device. Rose looked anxiously over at the Doctor. He took her hand. Jacob pressed the device to Rose's forehead and there was a tiny click.

That click was the strangest sensation Rose had ever felt, stranger even than being separated from her body in the first place. In that second she felt totally connected to every part of herself, as if she had reached out for her heart and lungs and was holding them to her. Lene stepped back and Rose shook her head experimentally, half expecting it to topple down into the grass. But it stayed firm.

'Thanks,' said Rose. It sounded ludicrously inadequate.

Lene smiled back. Then she stumbled. Jacob caught her and supported her gently, trying to make her comfortable on the hard ground. Then he turned to the Doctor. 'You beat Chantal, Doctor. So you're cleverer than Chantal?'

The Doctor grinned nonchalantly. 'S'pose I must

be.'

Jacob pointed to Lene, her prone form picked out in the light shining from the TARDIS windows. 'Then cure my wife. I want her to live.'

The Doctor's face fell. 'I can't.'

'Doctor,' said Rose quietly. 'Can't or won't?'

The Doctor crossed over to Lene, set the sonic screwdriver to diagnostic mode and ran it over her body. 'There's nothing I can do,' he said. 'Her life's been massively prolonged by genetic restructuring. She had her ageing mechanism switched off. She's had about 400 transplants. But every system, no matter how hard you try, wears out in the end.'

'She's not just a system!' snarled Jacob. His first tears trickled down his face.

The Doctor couldn't answer.

Quilley came close to Jacob and held him. It was not one of Quilley's grandiose, theatrical gestures. He'd moved naturally, comforted Jacob because that was the human thing to do.

The Doctor nodded to Quilley and said quietly, 'I can't take you with me. I can't take you home.'

'It was never my home,' Quilley replied evenly. 'This is my home.' With a small gesture he indicated the deep forest. 'I'm going to live here, and die here.' Some of his grandness seemed to return. 'And I intend to feel every last sensation as I'm doing it.'

'The cave people,' said Rose. 'Go and join up with them.'

Quilley nodded his thanks to Rose for her advice. Then he looked her fur-bikinied body up and down and made an indescribably lustful noise.

'Oh, please,' said the Doctor. 'Now you've rediscovered human nature, can you hurry up and rediscover basic manners?'

'What are manners again?' asked Quilley.

But the Doctor and Rose were already stepping back into the TARDIS.

The woman at the front of the small function room settled her glasses on her nose. 'Good afternoon, everyone, my name is Lynette Coates. I am the Superintendent Registrar and I would like to welcome you all here today to celebrate the marriage of Anna Marie O'Grady and Das Dimitru.'

Jack looked across at the Doctor and Rose. The groom's side of the seating was empty but for them, alongside a huge Irish gaggle of O'Gradys. 'Next give me something hard to do,' he whispered.

After picking up Jack they'd jumped forward a couple of weeks to catch the wedding. The Doctor was leaning back in his chair, beaming. Jack was stretched out like a cat, looking pleased with himself. Rose couldn't take her eyes away from the linked hands of Das and his new wife. She thought back to Reddy and Ka, kissing in that quiet corner of the forest just before the humans attacked. They must have been killed.

Still. Quilley and all the others – Tillun, Nan, Sakka and her baby – had been dead for 28,000 years.

But now, through Das, just a piece of that strange wild world would live on.

*

And 28,000 years before, another wedding was taking place.

T. P. Quilley flinched as the priest slapped the Great Fish of Matrimony in his face and cried, 'Turn to the stone of Brelalla!'

As the sun hit the stone he looked across at his new wife. 'So I'm one of the Family now?'

Nan smiled back. 'You are, my love. Shame we couldn't have had a nicer day for it, ain't it?'

'Not to worry,' mumbled Quilley. 'It'll warm up in about another 23,000 years.'

He surveyed his new family. Tillun was teaching Jacob to make spears for fishing; Reddy and Ka were playing with Sakka's child while her mother took a rest; and the last Hy-Bractor was sitting by the fire, tearing off huge chunks of meat from the boar it had killed and handing them round. Occasionally it sniffed at a human, but then all Quilley needed to do was hold up the picture drawn by the Doctor to remind it of its instructions.

'And now I'm part of the Family,' said Quilley, 'grant me this request, my dear.' For effect he leaned in and kissed Nan on the cheek.

She quivered with pleasure. 'Anything for you, dear.'

'My special wedding guests –' he indicated Ka and the other Neanderthals – 'let them stay here, join the tribe.'

Nan looked suspicious for a moment – but when Quilley kissed her again she melted. 'I suppose so. For you.'

Quilley sighed. He couldn't change history. But he could help to make this small part of it more civilised – more *humane*.

ACKNOWLEDGEMENTS

Thanks to Russell T Davies for his inspiration and *Springhill*, Justin Richards for his understanding, Helen Raynor for her advice, Steven Moffat for his instant messages, Rupert Laight for eternal friendship, Tom McMillen for being New Friend, Chris Theodoridis for the xenical, all the Not Players, the Wifes and No. 1 Who fan The Peden, David S. Taylor for his Republican heart of stone, Marianne Colbran for load-sharing, Rebecca Levene for her patience and Mark Gatiss for his thick, evil and somehow *alive* fog.

Particular thanks for notes and suggestions go to the owner of Hetherington, on behalf of the Duchess of Gladstone and her lady-in-waiting, the Lady Petunia.

Next in the Doctor Who *50th Anniversary Collection*:

BEAUTIFUL CHAOS
GARY RUSSELL
ISBN 978 1 849 90518 3

The Doctor Who *50th Anniversary Collection*
Eleven classic adventures
Eleven brilliant writers
One incredible Doctor

Wilfred Mott is very happy: his granddaughter, Donna, is back home, catching up with family and gossiping about her journeys, and he has just discovered a new star and had it named after him. He takes the Tenth Doctor with him to the naming ceremony. But the Doctor soon discovers something else new, and worryingly bright, in the heavens – something that is heading for Earth. It's an ancient force from the Dark Times.

And it is very, very angry…

An adventure featuring the Tenth Doctor, as played by David Tennant, and his companion Donna Noble.